Another Outlaw in the West

Joshua M. Turk

Joshua Tree
Publishing

• Chicago •

Another Outlaw in the West
Joshua M. Turk

Published by

Joshua Tree Publishing
• Chicago •
JoshuaTreePublishing.com

13-Digit ISBN: 978-1-941049-36-5

Front Cover Image Credit: © Jim

Disclaimer:
This book is designed to provide information about the subject matter covered. The opinions and information expressed in this book are those of the author, not the publisher. Every effort has been made to make this book as complete and as accurate as possible. However, there may be mistakes both typographical and in content. Therefore, this text should be used only as a general guide and not as the ultimate source of information. The author and publisher of this book shall have neither liability nor responsibility to any person or entity with respect to any loss or damage caused or alleged to be caused directly or indirectly by the information contained in this book.

Printed in the United States of America

A Drifter, A Hero, A Dream

In the year of 1882, a small group of individuals shaped part of our nation's history. In the decades that followed, our history books had nothing more than a paragraph detailing these events. Students were left to memorize and immortalize those that had been a canon of truth and righteous. The individuals have long since passed beyond memory, but this tale is what really happened.

Chapter 1

The wind blew hard from the west. It kept kicking up dust along the road, almost like a fog. On the road, was a man on his horse. The two continued on, and the mule carrying his supplies followed them. He had ridden some hundred and fifty miles in the past week and only three more separated him from his destination. The train would leave soon, but this did not change his speed. Either he would make it, or he wouldn't.

As he continued on, he looked out over the vast prairie around him, and the hills behind him in the distance. There was no noise besides the sound of the horse's hooves hitting the ground and the rustle of grass from the wind. He only thought about the train and of the drink he would buy before the train. None of where he came from would be hard to leave behind.

Soon he reached the outskirts of the town. The square-framed buildings rose next to each other. You could tell the age of each unpainted building by the faded color of the wood boards. Many had white washed the slats to hide it as each store owner tried to keep up with appearances. Everywhere there was dust from the drought. He passed by the church on his right. It had three large windows on the side of the church with very clear glass panes. He could see the altar from his horse and the cross behind it. After the church, he saw a doctor's office. Next to it was a lawyer's office with a dark red and white sign. It read "The Law Offices of Otis Scott." This road brought him to the main street. He slowed the horse as they made their way toward the railroad station at the end of the main street. The station was made of large wood rail slats. Outside the businesses, he noticed the horse troughs. The street was busy with men, farmers, travelers, women, and children. There was going to be a festival the next week for the town's twenty-year anniversary. He made his way through the crowd until he saw the ticket office. He pulled left on the reins to lead the horse toward it. Before reaching the ticket office, he saw a saloon. He rode up to it and got off his horse. He made a point not to let his spurs catch in the stirrup and tied the reins of both animals to the post in front of the saloon. He turned and walked inside. The oils chandeliers hung from the ceiling. The billiards table had a torn green cloth on it and sat dusty in the far corner. He approached the bar.

"What'll it be mister?" the bartender asked.

The man leaned onto the bar and replied, "Whatever ale you have and some whiskey." He looked around the room again. He noticed a group of men off to his left. He could tell they were a part of some gang based on the band they wore on their arm.

"It'll have to be whiskey then, we are out of ale." he said. The bartender turned behind him and grabbed a bottle of whiskey and a glass. He set down the glass, took the cork out of the whiskey bottle, and poured. "Haven't seen you around town before, what brings you in?" The glass had dust on the outside of it.

The man drank the whiskey down in one gulp and pushed the glass forward to signal for another pour. "Catching the train."

The bartender was intrigued. "You mean you aren't in town for the festival? Shame for that, people are coming from all over to celebrate. Even gonna have fireworks I hear."

"Afraid fireworks won't be enough to keep me," the man replied. He looked out the windows back to the street to watch the horse and the mule. "Where is the ticket office located? I didn't see one at the station."

"You'd be right. Some dumb bastard put it across the street. Thought it would keep the wires from getting cut." He poured another shot of whiskey, and the man paid for his drinks. He drank down the second glass just as quickly as the first.

As he put the change back in pocket, he said, "I am looking to get rid of my mule outside. He is strong and in fair health, where could I trade him?"

The bartender raised his eyebrows because the request caught him by surprise.

"My mule didn't make it through the winter. I might be willing to take him off your hands. You said he's outside, let me have a look?"

The man led the bartender outside. The bartender placed his hands on his hips as he looked at the mule.

"Yeah, I would say he is in pretty fine shape. What are you looking for him?"

"Seventy-five dollars, a bottle of whiskey, and you can keep the shovel, ax, and that old rifle. I'll keep the sandal bags."

"Seventy-five is a fair price," the bartender said. "Would you take seventy? It's all I have?"

The man looked at him and then the horse. He only wanted $65 but didn't want to seem too eager. He read the bartender's eyes. They had not twitched, he couldn't detect a lie in his voice. "Deal." He extended his arm and shook the bartender's hand. They went back into the saloon, and the bartender went into the back room behind the bar and came out with a folded piece of paper. The man took it and unfolded it. Inside the fold was the seventy dollars.

The group of men with sashes tied to their arms watched all this unfold. They looked at the money with the eyes of a beast. The leader of the group, Henry, whispered amongst the group. They were dusty, dirty, and smelled bad enough that even if the saloon hadn't been empty, everyone else would have sat at the other end.

The bartender turned around and grabbed a bottle of whiskey and handed it to the man. "Thanks for the business mister, good luck wherever you are headed."

The man tipped his cap as he walked out with the whiskey and money. He left the saloon and looked to his right down the street. A few stores down across the street, he saw a gunsmith's sign hanging over a door. The sign read "Holland's Gun Shop" on it. He stepped down onto the dusty street and made his way past some children playing off the boardwalk. They paid him no attention. He walked with a slight limp and opened the door. As he entered, he saw a clerk standing behind a glass counter.

"Good day sir," the clerk said to him without looking up from his papers.

The man nodded and said, "What rifles do you have?"

The clerk lifted his head up from the paper. He wore a dark overcoat that sat on top of his white collared shirt. He adjusted his glasses and said. "Well, I have five Henry rifles and several Winchesters in stock. They are located in that display over there next to the revolvers." He pointed behind the man.

The man turned around and walked over to the display case. It had a large metal lock on it. The glass case had not been cleaned.

"How is the 1882? The new model?" he asked.

The clerk responded, "I have sold three of those, have heard no complaints about that model."

"Is that a Winchester 1873?" the man said with surprise as he leaned further back over the case. This was the gun that he had to own. His uncle gave him one just like it many days before. This one looked worn, beaten, and scared. The wood on the butt looked like walnut.

"It is, sir." the clerk said as he was counting the money in the register. "The wood is walnut, which was rare at that time."

"Does it shoot straight?" the man asked. He smiled once he knew it was walnut.

"As an arrow, sir," the clerk replied. He had walked over to the case to join him as he sensed he had a buyer on his hands.

"How much?" the man asked as he looked at the clerk.

"That one costs thirteen dollars, it is slightly used," the clerk responded after he figured out which model the man was talking about.

"I will need cartridges, about a hundred," the man requested.

"That will bring the total to seventeen dollars," the clerk said.

The man paid him after the clerk took the gun out of the case. He held it and cocked it before giving him the money. He put the rounds in a small burlap sack. "If you don't mind me asking sir, why do you wear a gun belt for two guns, but only have one gun?"

"I haven't found the other one that caught my eye," the man said as he exited the store.

"I have these fine pistols right here," the clerk said eagerly.

"I could see how straight this thing shoots right now if you keep pushing," he said, turning back to the clerk.

The clerk looked concerned and apologized to him.

The man didn't laugh because he was not joking. He nodded and exited out into the street carrying the new rifle in his right hand. A new rifle will do some good he thought. The old one wasn't reliable past fifty yards.

He walked down the boardwalk again to his horse and placed the rounds into the saddle bags from the second horse and then threw it over his shoulder. His gun belt sagged down on his right hip because of this imbalance from only having one gun. The rifle he balanced on his shoulder as he walked across the street toward the ticket office. When he was just about to step up onto the porch of the ticket office, a man riding a horse almost ran him over. It almost caused him to drop his new rifle. The burly man on the horse cussed at him after he past him.

A woman on the steps of the ticket office said to him, "Looks like he was in hurry."

Amused, he said to her, "I have no idea where the days went when people didn't speak their mind unless spoken to." She huffed at his cold remark and turned away. He bent down and picked up the rifle. He swung open the door and stepped inside. There were two people in line before him. The line moved fast enough, and he bought himself a ticket. It cost two-fifty. He walked back out and stopped on the porch of the ticket station.

Still standing there, the woman from before gave him a dirty look. He walked over to her and said, "It seems like you don't know when a man is horsing around or when he's serious."

"That was real rude of you mister. How's a woman to know when a man is serious?" she asked.

"When he's holding a gun pointed in your general direction," he said with a smile.

With that comment, she laughed, and they said good day.

He walked back to his horse. He placed the rifle into its holster hooked onto the saddle. He untied the reins from the post and led the horse down the street. The men from inside the bar had been waiting for him and walked after him.

"I think you might want to give me that rifle and the money." Henry said to him. He wore a blue shirt and white hat. He had a cigarette in his mouth. Three men stood behind him.

The man said back to Henry, "You trying to buy another sash for your other arm?" He kept walking without addressing the man in blue.

"We got a funny guy gents," he said to the group of men and they laughed. He yelled, "Hey yellow belly, you don't come into my town without paying a fee unless you want trouble." They aloud said they agreed with him.

Thomas, one of the posse, yelled, "He don't seem to be listening too good."

"No, he don't, we ought to whoop 'em," Henry said back to him.

"I must have missed the sign," the man said as he kept walking toward the train. He was about fifty feet from the boarding station.

From inside the general store, the sheriff could see the dispute beginning to form. He had tried to keep Henry and his Bandits in check for some time. He put down the candy he was trying to buy for his sweet tooth and began to make his way outside. The clerk of the store shook his head. He had seen this before, usually ended with a coffin or two.

Henry loved to start gun fights; he was a drifter and gambler. Luckily, the man just kept walking, and this infuriated Henry. This caused the sheriff to relax as he stood outside the general store. The man and his horse were almost to the station. Henry walked faster to catch him, with the men behind him, and hit the horse on hind legs to startle it. The horse neighed the first time, but the man just kept walking.

"You're gonna give me the rifle and the money," Henry yelled. The man stopped walking as he had just about reached the platform of the boarding station. Henry drew his gun and shot in front of the horse's feet. It neighed and rose its front legs.

The man had enough and said, "I wouldn't make me miss my train." The posse did not laugh this time. The man turned around and let go of the reins. The horse stopped walking. It had seen this before.

Henry laughed again and shot in front of the horse's legs again, causing it to raise its front legs. He holstered his gun. "Give me that rifle and the money—or the next one's aimed at you!"

The man smiled at him and shook his head from side-to-side.

"You seem like a crack shot," the man said back to the bandits.

The sheriff saw the men behind Henry lower their hands close to their pistols. He thought to himself, we will need one more casket. The crowd ran from the men and a few seconds went by. The five-minute warning whistle blew from the train. The men stared at each other for a few seconds.

Henry said after the whistle, "Looks like you won't be catching that train." He went to draw his gun because he had holstered it after firing at the horse. Four-gun shots rang out, and four men hit the ground. Henry and his posse lay crumpled in street. Smoke poured out of one pistol. It was a long barrel Colt in the hand of the man. Henry lay on the ground still breathing. Two were moaning in pain as they were about to expire. One had died already. The man walked over to Henry, a bullet had gone through his chest. He looked at the bandit's revolver next to him. It was a Colt just like his except it had a shorter barrel and slightly darker shade of nickel, almost like a cobalt. The man knelt down and dusted it off as he picked it up. He put it in the empty holster on his left hip. He looked back at the bandit on the ground. The man pointed his gun at him. Henry looked up at the gun barrel, then up at the man's face. He trembled and pissed himself.

He took a deep breath and exhaled and said with a smirk, "I told you I was gonna make this train crack shot." He shot him through the forehead. Still standing over the body, he began reloading his revolver. First, by letting the shell casing fall onto Henry's body, and second, by placing a new bullet in the chamber.

The sheriff had stood still terrified at what he had seen. He shook himself off the platform and walked out toward the man. The sheriff had his hand on his gun. The sheriff said to him, "You are under arrest." The man had just finished reloading his revolver, spun the cylinder and looked up at him. His cold eyes locked with the sheriffs. Neither said anything, they didn't have to.

The horse had not moved. He grabbed the reins and holstered his reloaded revolver. The man turned with his horse and stepped up onto the wood platform. The sheriff's mouth opened to protest, but nothing came out. Finally, the sheriff said, "What is your name son?"

The man turned back around, "Everett Gunn."

The sheriff nodded.

Gunn turned back, and he walked over to the train, loaded his horse in the stable car, and took his seat with the bottle of whiskey. He filled his flask with some and put the bottle into the saddle bag he carried.

The woman from outside ticket shop had wandered closer to the bodies on the street where the fight had happened. The woman next to her said, "I overheard him say he had a train to catch, and then he drew his gun."

The women from the ticket shop said to her, "I guess he meant it."

Chapter 2

It had been several hours since he had boarded the train in the town. The sun beat down on the cars. They had opened the windows to let out air, but it made no difference. The train traveled through plains with tall grass, and pheasants and other birds darted from their protective cover at the sound of the engine. Further out, they could see the last remaining buffalo in the area grazing. Magnificent animals he thought to himself.

Gunn slumped in his seat and faced outside the windows of the train car. His lower back had the same dull pain it had for years and ran down the back of his leg. The dark green paint inside the car began to annoy him. He closed his eyes to doze off, and when he woke, he took out a flask to drink. He had filled the flask from the whiskey bottle several times already. He took a pocket watch out from an internal pocket on the right side of his duster jacket. He opened it and looked at it for a long time, running his thumb along the outer frame tracing it. He finally closed it and went back to looking out the window.

A few more hours passed, and the grass was drying out and turning brown as if it would turn into sand at almost any moment. This drought had been talked about for weeks. It made the farmers anxious for their crops. The sign for the town of Cold Creek appeared on the side of the tracks. It was a mining town; some silver and a little gold had been found in the streams around there. The mines caused the town to boom quickly. A jolt of excitement jumped into the passengers. Gunn simply adjusted his back. The train's pace slowed as the brakes were applied. The train crawled into the station until it came to a halt. The train had ten cars in total, one for animals, two for cargo, five for passengers, and the rest for speed and power. He had sat in the fourth car, which had remained empty because everyone was afraid to sit near him after witnessing him kill four men.

As the train sat in the station, he took out the new pistol from his holster and admired it. There was a phrase carved into the barrel, "May the light of heaven shine on your grave." It was an old Irish blessing he recognized. He laughed at the irony. The sheen from the dark-colored metal soothed him. He had seemingly gotten it for the price of five bullets, but he had to risk his life to do. This had made him laugh too. He looked out and saw that the buildings all had fresh coats of paint on them, fresh wood shingles, and no faded colors anywhere. The train station had flat and even wood slats and comfortable sitting benches.

Soon all the cargo and passengers had boarded the train. No new passengers had entered his car. The conductor yelled, "All aboard!" The train began to crawl along the tracks as it moved away from the town and gained speed. After it picked up speed, the trip seemed the same as before. Gunn pulled a cigarette out of his pocket and lit it with a match. Suddenly, a young woman entered the car he sat in and sat across from him. She did not know of the killing that had taken place before because she had boarded in Cold Creek. She had on a dark dress and wore a white round hat. He smiled to the woman across from him and tipped his hat. She politely nodded back and turned toward the window to not invite any unnecessary conversation.

He decided to say something about her dress and opened his mouth when a gunshot ran out, and then another from the cars closer up to the engine car. People began to scream on the train. The woman sitting across from Gunn began to turn white in a panic.

Gunn said to himself, "This has turned out to be an interesting day."

He stood up and peered through the window in the door into the car that was in front of theirs. There he could see a man running his way and another chasing him. This man ran into his car and to the other door. The other door was locked when he tried the handle, and the man then turned back. His face had sharp angles and a red hue from the sun. He looked frightened. Through the open door to their car, a man with a gun stepped forward. He pointed it at the scared man and took another step forward past the man sitting in the car.

Gunn sat in his seat, looked over, and saw the woman begin to scream. There was blood running down her arm as one of the bullets had caught her in the upper arm. Her face became white as she looked at the arm. She took her other hand and used it to put pressure on the wound. The people in the car ahead of theirs screamed and wailed. Gunn was still holding the new pistol he had just taken from his duel.

The man with the red hued faced begged, "Don't shoot! Don't shoot! We can work something out here." The man that had been chasing him, still held his gun and pointed it at him.

As he pointed the pistol, he said, "You son of a bitch!"

Right as the man went to pull the trigger, Gunn stood up. Gunn hit him over the head with the butt of the new pistol. This caused him to fire wide, and the bullet shot through a window, shattering the glass onto a seat. The man in red did not topple over, so Gunn hit him again, harder this time. This knocked out the man in red, and blood was running down his face from a cut on his head. It did not stain his shirt but did stain his cream-colored bandanna he wore around his neck.

Gunn wiped his nose with the back of his hand that was still holding the pistol. He turned to the woman and said, "Let me see your arm." The woman still screamed uncontrollably, and he moved her hand away from the wound. The bullet had passed through; she would get to keep her arm he thought. He holstered his gun and took her scarf and tied a tourniquet. The well-dressed man with the reddish hued face walked over to help him bandage her as he tied it.

"Let me help. Thank you for saving my ass there," he said to Gunn. After they had her arm tended, he turned and tied up the man who had tried to shoot him. He picked up his gun from the car floor and threw out the train window. A railroad worker came in and began asking questions about the incident to passengers in the car for the coming arrest in the next town.

"What is your name?" the railroad worker said to the man who had almost been shot. He wore a dark uniform but had on no name tag.

"You provide insurance against reprisals?" Gunn snapped back as he sat there helping the woman.

"What do you mean?" the railroad worker said back to him confused.

"I didn't think so. All you need to know is that this guy started shooting at that guy, and I stepped in and put that guy on the floor. Get this woman off at the next town to see a doctor."

"But sir, I need a statement from you," the attendant demanded.

"You just got one. I would write that down."

He got up and walked past him to his seat. The first man followed him and sat across from Gunn. After the attendant exited, he closed the door to the car. No other passengers would enter. It was just the two men.

"Where are you headed?" the man dressed in a suit said.

"End of the line, plans are open ended." Gunn replied. He didn't expect the conversation to continue.

"Open ended, that sounds exciting," asked the man in the suit.

"With shit like that, it damn well could be," Gunn said back to him.

"That is true. Do have any plans for employment at the end of the line?" the man asked him.

"I do not." He replied.

"I see, open prospects. Well, do you like money?"

Everett quipped. "I do, who doesn't?"

The man in the suit leaned in and said, "Exactly! The more important question is do you *love* money? See, I *love* money. I aim to collect it. You see, it is the antidote to life's problems." He paused to judge Gunn's level of curiosity. When he saw he had him nodding, he continued, "The difficulty . . . I find, is obtaining enough money to solve these problems?"

"I don't have an answer to that," Gunn said showing his disinterest as he began to turn away from him.

The man in the suit placed his hand on his chest as he said, "I do have one and a great practice to acquire it. I happen to work for a certain individual, or really a company, that acquires particular producers of wealth that are in a state of shall we say shit."

"Why would anyone want to work in shit," Gunn asked.

"It is not in shit literally, but despair."

"Despair doesn't sound much better that shit," Gunn replied.

The well-dressed man now felt he had the attention of the man and continued on, "My name is Vernon Deib. Nice to make your acquittance."

"Everett Gunn."

They shook hands in the train car.

Vernon continued, "Now, about this state of despair we were talking about. These businesses that are acquired by this company do not carry the value that they otherwise would if say, a sophisticated or even well-connected benefactor had been responsible for them in the first place. One could argue then and reach the conclusion that in a way, these apparatuses in shit, despair what have you, should be in the hands and truly belong to individuals that can take full advantage of the opportunity that exists within them?"

"I suppose so," Gunn said back to him. "Hell of a point of view to justify robbing people."

"Well, if you agree then, isn't it in everyone's best interest to get these into the possession of the well-connected and well informed as quickly as possible?" Vernon suggested.

"I reckon so. That is a powerful sermon you got there. Again, sounds an awful like stealing though," Gunn replied.

"It is not stealing, when you are repossessing something that has delinquent accounts on it, money owed."

"There is good money in that?" he asked. "Muscle end of that business."

Nodding his head fiendishly as his eyes narrowed, he whispered, "There is. Lots of it in fact. Enough money to make life's problems fade away."

Gunn was curious and interested.

"So what do you do for this company? I ain't have much education. Seems like you have a bit, using a bunch of fancy words there."

"You seem pretty schooled with that revolver there. As for me, I have been educated at some of the finest schools we have in this country but can't shoot for shit. Naturally, the transfer of this shit from one side to the other often gets quite messy. All the writing and reading skills in the world don't mean shit when someone starts shooting at you."

"That's the truth."

Vernon continued, "Quite right. No one wants to transfer or lose their operation or livelihood because it is a defeat of a person's pride. Pride is a terrible thing. Now, I act as the pressure and apply the leverage needed to complete these transactions. As you just witnessed on this train. People don't like to part with their shit."

"What is your role then in it?"

"I am merely a courier, a janitor, a servant of the people who specializes in the collection and transfer of ownership in shit to individuals who can harness value of it. For which I receive an agreeable sum."

"You are in shit?" Gunn asked.

"Waste deep, and it glorious," Vernon said.

"How is business?"

"You see the frontier," the man pointed out the window, "that is how much opportunity exists. If you can harness it." He closed his fist and then paused, "Which is why, currently, I could use someone to help me maximize my services. As you can see from this incident, my services can irritate those who feel they are being deprived of their shit. A few more close calls and my employer will be in need of a more permanent replacement." He paused again, looked at Gunn, and placed his hand next to the bag he was carrying on the seat next to them. "Judging by your involvement in my situation here today, I think you would perform quite well." He turned and kicked the man tied up on the floor as he started to awaken.

"When can I start?" Everett said.

"Promptly," Vernon replied.

"So, I am gonna get to shoot someone?"

Everett took out a flask of whiskey and raised the flask up. He had forgotten it was empty and shook it to confirm it was empty. Regrettably, he put it back in his pocket.

"Most definitely. Here have some of mine," Vernon said back to him with complete confidence as Everett was taking out his flask. Vernon took out a shiny flask with an engraving on it and took a drink. He wiped his mouth after he finished. He held out the flask to Everett. Gunn took a long pull. It was sweet and a liquor he had not had before. He handed it back to him.

"What is this?" Gunn asked him.

"Cognac, some of the finest money can buy."

The train continued on the track heading to its destination. The train car had returned to normal after the incident. A security guard entered their car sometime later and sat in the car on the other end watching Vernon and Everett. He felt satisfied that neither of them meant any of the patrons any trouble. The two men had continued talking about a manner of subjects. Everett felt curious to ask one more question.

"If all the property is transferring to the corporation, how do you get paid?" Everett asked.

Vernon laughed to himself. He crossed his leg and put his ankle on the other knee. He put his hand up to his face and rested his chin on it. "There is a regular wage but also, not all the property makes it through the transfer. This is understood by our employer that there will be some discrepancies in their inventory."

"Discrepancies, amounting to how much?" Gunn asked.

"Thousands of dollars. How else would I afford cognac and an Italian suit?" Vernon replied.

Both men laughed.

"Italian must be expensive," Gunn said back.

The train reached the station. Both men stood up as it came to a crawl and stopped. The passengers on the train all stood up who were getting off. The train whistle blew, and it was a frenzy stepping out onto the wood planks that acted as a platform. Both men walked down to the animal car and waited as their horses were walked off onto the platform.

The sun was setting, but the sky was cloudy. There was a half moon rising.

Chapter 3

Gunn rode his horse to the left of Vernon. The animals jogged along the road. Both men stood tall in the stirrups to make it as comfortable as possible. The road was rougher than what he had grown accustomed to back home. The rocks were larger, and it was bumpier than he was accustomed to. The sky had a red and orange hue out to the west. It would be getting dark soon enough, and Vernon had not decided if they would make for the town or to make camp. Neither man had spoken for over an hour. The moon had come out in the sky before dark. It was a crescent moon. It all made no difference to Gunn as he kept smoking his cigar.

He just kept his focus on the sun as it began setting off in the distance over the horizon. A wooded area lay not too far up ahead, and Vernon appeared to be slowing down his horse. Gunn thought this would be where they would make camp tonight. The trees looked like a painter's pigment thrown on a painting. There were pine, birch, willows, and cedar trees throw about in a manner that did not make sense. They blocked out the sun and were so thick that the forest floor had nothing growing on it.

The sun had fully set when they reached the thicket, and the temperature began to get drop rapidly. The sky grew darker, and the stars began to appear as if they were new born in the sky. The air stung their bare flesh, and when they breathed, they could see their breath. Gunn put on his jacket to keep himself warm after he tied his horse to a tree. He opened one of his saddle bags. The leather felt cold and stuck to his hand. He took out some grain and unloaded his blanket. The horse ate the grain in large gulps. Vernon kept watch out into the woods. Gunn laid out his blanket onto the ground. He took his rope and spread that around his sleeping blanket to keep snakes away. Neither man had spoken to the other since camp had started. Both waited to see who would crack first.

An owl sounded in the distance, and they heard the rustle of leaves every so often. Gunn used his cigar to spark some of the dry brush he had collected from around the camp. He found that dried out pine cones kept fires going and also threw them onto the coals to get it burning hot. The orange, red, and blue flame danced back and forth as it brought definition to each of their face's features in the darkness. It cast a wide light across the wood. Within a few minutes, the fire grew strong and high.

Gunn's hands felt stiff from the cold at night. His gloves didn't change this, and he rubbed his hands together for a minute or two to loosen them up. Then he opened his saddle bag to take out some jerky to eat. He kept on flexing his hands towards the fire to bring feeling back to them.

"Is that still agreeable?" the Vernon asked as he was watching out over the woods.

"Find out for yourself," Gunn said back to him as he extended a piece with his knife that he had just cut.

Vernon turned toward him and extended his hand. He took the piece of jerky and sat on the other side of the fire. He smelled it first and then took a bite, chewed and swallowed. "It's tough, but agreeable." He took another bite. "Preferable to going hungry out here in the cold." He finished the last bite and reached for another piece. The two men sat eating the jerky for a few minutes as the fire kicked heat out onto each of them. The wood popped and threw sparks towards them.

"So, what is . . ." Gunn began to say.

Vernon interrupted him. "You are eager for your first job, that is good. You will know momentarily." He turned toward Gunn and locked eyes with him. He had a cold stare and cocky expression on his face. He finished chewing the jerky and swallowed it. He did not want to repeat himself, so he spoke clearly. "We have an acquisition tomorrow. Collecting an overdue payment due our employer and legal documents to their land. I will sit and make the exchange with two men, a Mr. Boughton and a Mr. Celler, tomorrow inside the hotel lobby. Boughton has a temper. If he feels cheated, and you can be certain that he will, these two and six other men are going to have quite a dissent from our position on the matter. That may complicate our return."

Gunn sat there soaking in every word as he saw the fire illuminate Louis' face. He spoke candidly and without expression. "You will be across from me at the bar facing the table. My back will be to the bar. Do not use your name, do not speak or reference me in anyway. Should either of these gentlemen escalate their actions, proceed without restraint."

"Without restraint," Gunn repeated.

"Yes, without restraint," Vernon said.

"Sounds like a good time," Gunn said calmly.

Both men laughed. Vernon tossed Gunn a pocket watch, and Gunn caught it.

"We don't shoot first unless they draw, but we finish it. How is your repeater?" Vernon asked.

"Just bought this '73, it'll work do the job," he answered.

"Unproven rifle makes me nervous, but good, I am meeting these gentlemen at one in the afternoon. I will ride the extra horse into town before you in the morning. I will ride with him to take care of some of the finer details. You will stay here. A black wagon will arrive at half past ten to pick you up. Leave both horses tied here with the driver of the wagon. A mister Johnson, Clarence Johnson will be driving it."

"Is he with us?" Gunn interrupted.

Vernon responded, "He is a trusted partner. Now, you will leave the wagon behind the general store in the town. Mr. Johnson has kindly fitted his wagon with two shotguns and shells that are disguised on the right side of the wagon. Leave them there. Upon your arrival, proceed directly to the hotel."

"Alright," Gunn said back to him with several nods. He laid down and looked up to the sky before putting his hat over his head.

"It never goes as planned, Gunn. No matter how simple," Vernon said before he went to sleep.

Vernon pulled his blanket over him and rolled over onto his side. Everett pulled his blanket to his neck to cover himself and turned the opposite way. He kept his hand on revolver. He did his best to try and fall asleep. Soon he heard Vernon snoring fast asleep over the crackle of the fire. Everett felt anxious and tossed and turned from side to side. The howl of coyotes in the distance carried from the distance.

The next morning Gunn arose from his sleep. He shook his head. He looked around, and there was no noise except the crackling of a fire. He rubbed his tightened fists into his eyes to wake up. He sat up and saw a man he did not recognize leaning over the fire He heard the sizzle of something cooking and the smell of grease. The aroma careened over to his nose and made his mouth water.

"Hey yah, fella. I'm Johnson. How do you like your bacon?" Mr. Johnson asked. He was wearing a black top hat that had a hole in it, a green vest that had no buttons on it over a white shirt and reddish pants. He had a shotgun propped against a tree by the horses to the right. There was a kettle of coffee next to the fire.

"Soggy. I didn't think we would have time for breakfast."

He sat up and dusted his clothes off. He rolled up his blanket and checked his revolvers. He took a piss away from the camp between two ferns. When he finished, he walked back over the fire. The bacon looked good as the grease bubbled on top of it. "Is that ready yet?" His mouth was watering. He had not eaten bacon for several months. He couldn't wait to have a taste.

"Oh, you thought this was for you?" Mr. Johnson replied with a laugh. "You don't have time for breakfast." Johnson kept laughing.

"Then why did you ask?" Gunn sounded with a raised eyebrow.

"Just to give you shit." He laughed hard and hit his leg. "You are running late anyway." He pointed behind Gunn through the trees to a wagon with horses. "Take the wagon about 100 yards to the road, head south for five miles. You best be in a hurry. He hates it when people are late."

Gunn cursed him under his breathe. He asked him the time, and the man looked down at the watch.

"You have almost an hour and a half to get there."

"Shit," Gunn said. He went to the wagon and took the reins. He whipped the reins and yelled at the horses. The dirt under their hooves kicked up, and they pulled the wagon along. He did not want to disappoint Vernon on their first job together. His stomach groaned for the bacon, and he cursed Mr. Johnson for teasing him over the bacon as he rode away. He could still smell it in the air but took his mind off it. He knew one thing: he was going be shooting someone by the end of the day. It even might be Mr. Johnson. The wagon bounced along on the round. Gunn pulled back on the reins, so an axle wouldn't break on the wagon. He continued at a slower pace for the last two miles. His rifle lay next to him in the front seat, and his pistols each were in their holster.

The town appeared in the distance. First, it appeared as a small dot on the horizon. Then, slowly the buildings came into focus and detail until he reached the main street. When he reached the main street, he could make out the sign above the hotel that had been freshly painted white and red. It stuck out compared to the worn, dull wood planks of the hotel whose paint had faded. The main street held most of its traffic at the far end where several different shops existed. The washing and bath house seemed the most crowded on that day. He took the wagon down the street and secured the wagon behind the general store. As he walked through an alley to the main street, the people in the town peered at him suspiciously. He tried not to wear his frustration on his face, but he couldn't blend in. He looked down at his watch instead of the one that Vernon had given him and laughed because he knew it was not correct.

He turned and took the final few paces before entering the hotel. It was three stories tall, much taller than typical hotels he had seen. The clock on the wall showed he was fifteen minutes late. He walked past the cigar Indian statue and into the common eating area. There were swinging doors that separated this room, and he pushed them open. To his right, he saw Vernon facing him with two gentlemen's backs to him. Vernon gave him a peculiar look, and he could see the rage in his eyes in that glance. The two gentlemen turned and looked at him as he continued over to the bar and sat down. He took the seat closest to the back on the other side of the bar. The bartender, a portly fellow with a magnificent beard asked him what he wanted.

"Just a pint." Gunn said.

The bartender walks over to the tap, grabs a mug, washes it quickly with a rag, and then pours the beer from the tap into the mug. There was just the right amount of head from the pour.

"Where are you from sir?" he asked.

"From up north." He took the glass and tasted the beer. It was terrible, but most beer tasted terrible in this part of the country during this time of year. He wanted that damn bacon. He took another sip.

"What brings you to town?" he asked back as he leaned on the bar hoping to engage in conversation. "That accent doesn't sound like from up north?"

"Just passing through, going to visit my brother," he said back rather calmly. He took another sip. "I have traveled all over."

"We don't get many folks passing through. Just have miners and farmers out here. Ranchin' been tough for them though, with the drought this year," the bartender thrust into the conversation.

"Hard times for everybody it seems," Gunn replied dryly, trying to act engaged while keeping his wits about himself.

"Yes," the bartender said back. "You want some breakfast, we got eggs."

"Well, I hope it picks up and that sounds good," Gunn said back.

"Appreciate that mister. That will be a dime."

"Not a problem." He put down a dime. "Keep the rest of that."

Gunn looked around at the bar. There was a mirror behind the bar, white wallpaper with red and green stripes on the walls, and bronze oil lamps on the walls for lighting during the evening. To the right of the bar, on the rear wall was a painting of a mountain scene. He looked over to the hunter and the two men. Their conversation seemed to be running smoothly, considering what it was they were discussing. All three men had a beer.

"That is a nice painting," he said to the bartender who was still interested in keeping a conversation. He motioned for another beer as well.

The bartender took his glass and filled it back up. "It brightens the place up a bit, I think. I like the lake reflection of the mountain. Almost like a mirror."

"It is. How long on those eggs?" Gunn asked. He placed the glass back in front of him. The rest of bar area and lobby was empty.

"Take about fifteen minutes, kitchen is backed up. So, are you in ranching, mining, or gunning fighting?" the bartender asked jokingly.

Gunn was amused by the joke but changed the subject. "This beer grows on you, it tastes like shit at first."

The bartender was surprised by his frankness but laughed in agreement.

"That ought to be our motto; the shit that grows on yah."

Gunn laughed and looked back to view Vernon's conversation. The conversation had become more testy, and one of the gentleman had just slammed his glass on the table. He was cursing and waving off the Vernon's comments.

The bartender leaned into Gunn and said softly, "I think those boys are in deep with that man. Probably owe him some money."

"You might be right, what are they ranchers . . . miners," Gunn asked.

"Ranchers, can tell by their clothes. I hope this gets resolved. I don't need more shenanigans after the brawl last week." He hesitated and then said, "I am going to give them a beer on the house. It might call them down."

"What happened last week?" Gunn asked

"Damn shoot out, the mirror behind me was replaced yesterday. Lucky the general store had two of 'em," the bartender said before walking over to offer the men the beers.

Gunn watched as the bartender walked over toward the table with the three men. All three men looked at him angrily as he put the beers on the table and said it was on the house. None of them said anything. The bartender realized he made a mistake and turned and went back behind the bar. None of the men said anything, as a cold silence took over the bar for a few seconds.

Vernon picked up his glass and took a long drink. Some of the residue remained on his mustache. The two men did not touch their beers. They reluctantly had to accept defeat on the issue at hand. They were both slouching now. Vernon looked at them and spoke again, then pointed upstairs with his right hand.

Gunn could not make out what they were saying, but he could see his partner holding his pistol in his right hand under the table as he pointed upstairs with his left. He then placed his hand holding the gun back on the table. This seemed to intimidate the men even more. One of them stood up and walked outside. The man looked over at Gunn and the bartender. He was clearly angry and defeated but had a crazy look in his eye. Gunn made brief eye contact with Vernon and then lowered his shooting hand to move his coat behind his holster. He stood up.

The man walked back in with a saddle bag on his shoulder and threw it on the table. Vernon, with his left hand, opened the bag and took out three pieces of paper and a stack of money. The loan payments and title to the land Everett thought.

"Holy shit! That is a lot of money," the bartender said rather loudly to Gunn.

"Mind your own business. That will get your mirror shot up again," Gunn snapped at him.

The bartender looked down at the glass he was cleaning after glancing quickly at the shiny new mirror.

"My apologies," he snorted back.

The two men sitting with Vernon had gotten up and left. Gunn ignored the bartender's remarked and instead just watched and waited. He had his hand on his revolver and tried to read the situation. Vernon stood up and left some money on the table for the bartender. He turned to the bartender and said, "That should cover it." He put the money and papers in the bag he had with him. He then put his pistol back into its holster and took two steps toward the bar. Neither made much eye contact with each other. Don't look like we are in cahoots Everett thought. He stayed still but moved freely. Like an eagle in the sky, smooth and graceful.

The two men had stormed out of the bar in a fit. There was one window in the front of the bar, and Gunn could see two men standing outside join the men that had just paid Vernon. Each was armed, and they turned around to enter the saloon. They carried two pistols and a rifles that he counted in his head. Gunn focused on the men approaching but kept breathing calmly.

"Shits about to get fun," he said to Vernon who had just reached the bar. Both men put their hands on their revolvers.

"Good, all their posturing started to bore me," Vernon replied with a laugh.

Gunn drew both pistols from his hips. Vernon spun around with a single long barrel colt. It was dark metal that matched his shirt. A man wearing a brown shirt aiming a shotgun at them had walked into the bar first. Gunn fired his left pistol into the man's left shoulder area. The man screamed, and he fired and missed both Gunn and Louis. The buckshot shattered the most expensive bottle of whiskey behind the bar. The glass ricocheted into the bottles and onto the floor behind the bar.

"Everybody get down!" the bartender hollered from behind the bar. The bartender grabbed his shot gun and stood up over the bar and went to fire at the men that had walked in. A bullet grazed his ear, and he fell back onto the floor.

"My ear! Dammit, damn you!" he bellowed.

Vernon laughed as the shootout continued.

"Better the ear than your cock old man."

Vernon returned fire as they were trying to use the tables as cover. Everett shot the man holding the shot gun again with his right pistol. The man fell over, and his breathing became labored. He tried to sit up to continue fighting.

They kept firing. Everett and Vernon worked their way over to the stair case. Gunn had shot one of the other men as well, and he crumpled to the ground holding his leg. This left the two cowards firing from behind tables. Several of the civilians had jumped to the floor but still were hit by either bullet or splitter fragments. This all happened in a manner of seconds. There was a short break as the men all began to reload their revolvers. Gunn and Vernon made their way over towards the staircase next to the bar. During the silence, people, who laid on the floor, screamed out for help.

A bullet grazed Gunn's shoulder that was fired through the window. Gunn had just finished reloading his short barrel colt and fired back through the glass. One of the panes shattered, and the pieces landed on the floor. Vernon and Gunn finally made it to the staircase.

At this point, Vernon pointed his dark revolver at the mirror and fired. The bullet shattered the glass. The sound bounced off the walls and caused more screams out of the patrons.

"You fucking bastard. Not the mirror. Fuck, not the mirror," the bartender said as Vernon went up the staircase first and kept firing down below into the room. Bullets whizzed by in several directions. The bartender stood up and shot one of the men in the back with his shotgun. Gunn shot the other man chasing them through the neck, and he feel backwards drowning on his own blood.

"Watch behind us," Vernon said as it appeared they had cleared the room besides the bartender who fired his next shot at them, missing only because he slipped on the alcohol on the floor. He led them up to the third floor. They paused here for a moment and reloaded their pistols.

"You really wanted to shoot that mirror didn't you," Gunn said with a laugh.

"Yeah, he just didn't know when to shut up," Vernon said back. They could hear the footsteps of the men a floor below starting to make their way up the stairs.

"Hurry," Vernon said as he kicked open a door to a room that overlooked the high steeple roof. "After you," he said to Everett.

Everett didn't speak and jumped out the window with his pistols in both hands. He did his best to not tighten his grip but couldn't relax. He remembered the shots through the window came from men across the street. He fell onto his back and began to slide down the roof. He didn't yell or scream. The worn wood shingles didn't send any splinters into his skin. He kept his focus on the street as bullets whizzed past him as he tried to return fire at the two men across the street firing at him. His shorter pistol jammed, and the other he managed a shot at one of them. It was close enough that the man ducked for cover behind some barrels.

He heard Vernon sliding down behind him. Everett slid right off the edge of the roof. He landed in the back of the wagon he had parked behind the saloon. He dropped the short pistol that had jammed into the back of the wagon. He gathered himself onto the driver's seat and grabbed the reins with his one free hand. Vernon missed the wagon and tumbled onto the ground. He got up and climbed into the back of the wagon. Bullets whizzed past them from both directions. He opened up the side compartment and grabbed the two, double barrel shot guns. He tossed one to Everett who took it in his right hand after he holstered his pistol.

He turned around and whipped the reins. This signaled to the horses to take off. Vernon kept his eyes on their rear. Four men came out from the front and began to fire at them. The bullets flew by. Vernon returned fire and dropped two men.

"It's like pheasant hunting back home," he yelled. "You alright?"

"Just a splinter in my ass," Gunn said. "I'll be fine."

"Keep it fast, push 'em hard." Vernon said.

Everett stayed quiet and did just that. The horses bolted forward; they could feel the air fly past their faces. Vernon reloaded his shotgun. Each yelled out in excitement. Everett looked back and could see the town getting smaller. They made it to the wooded area without any disturbance and knew they weren't going to be followed. It had taken almost an hour, but they had increased the distance and found safety. Everett loosed up on the reins, his knuckles white and burning from the gripping them so tightly past the point of exhaustion. The horses breathed heavily, and their hair blowing in the wind. They saw Mr. Johnson near the oak trees that had signs of their camp site.

"I see you made it," Johnson said to them.

The wagon came to a stop.

"You knew we would," Vernon said.

"That I did," Johnson replied. "I fed your horses and have them ready for you."

"Excellent," Vernon said. "How was your breakfast?"

"I enjoyed it," Johnson replied. "Still full actually." He began to take the horses out of their rigging to tie them to a tree to feed them.

"I bet you did," Everett said with a hint of sarcasm that coated his words like melted butter coats a piece of warm toast.

As he got down from the back of the wagon, Vernon turned to Everett, "You were late. I was beginning to think you were not reliable." He winked at Johnson.

Gunn couldn't see this.

"He means nothing by it, Vernon. I cooked it in front of him and didn't share. He had to get going," he said to them.

Everett got down off the wagon.

"Well, he got there just in time," Vernon said while examining his suit jacket. There were two fresh bullet holes in it. "Closer than I would have liked."

"Just so you know," Everett said. "I'm a better shot with a full stomach. That will keep your clothes in good repair."

All the men laughed at this as Vernon showed Johnson the bullet holes in his jacket.

"Well then, I will be getting on my way," Johnson said to them. He walked over and shook their hands.

Vernon took out an envelope and gave it to him. "Tell the big man I say hello."

"I will pass that along," Vernon said.

Everett simply tipped his cap. There was respect there between the two as they stared into each other's eyes. The man jumped onto the wagon and began to ride away from them. Everett began to holster his rifle when he noticed Vernon take his rifle and aim at the man as he rode away. He pulled the trigger, and Mr. Johnson fell over as the wagon continued on the path.

Everett didn't question him but simply looked at Vernon half alarmed and surprised. He reached for his own pistol.

"Don't draw your iron. I got two rules. Don't ever mention our employer. That and don't be late. Breaking the first, you get killed," Vernon said as he peered in Everett's eyes.

Everett did not flinch. Vernon opened his inner jacket pocket and took out two cigars. He handed one to Everett. He lit a match and lit Everett's cigar first and then his own. He opened the bag he was carrying, and there were several thousand dollars inside of it. He gave three thousand to Everett.

Everett took the money and put it in his bill fold. "I don't ask questions, just tell me what to do and who I need to shoot at."

"Good, this will work out just fine then," he said to Everett. "Just be on time."

"Where we headed to next?" Everett asked.

"I need you in Ohio in a month's time, North of Cincinnati. There is a town called Mulberry. We will meet at the hotel on the 6th." He reached out and gave $1,000 to Gunn.

"I will see you then," Everett said with a nod.

He turned and rode off. His face still could not hide his excitement from the cash he held in his hand.

"Gunn, I told you the money's good. Don't spend it all at once," he said with a laugh.

What Everett Gunn didn't know is those ranching lands would be bringing in thousands more over the next several years to the company.

"I won't," he said with a smile.

He turned and road east. He was hungry for steak and eggs, and coffee. God, how he wanted a cup of coffee. The wagon could be heard riding aimlessly in the distance through the trees until it reached the clearing.

Chapter 4

The sun rose over the hills of Ohio near Cincinnati and Northern Kentucky. The light peaked through the tall trees and it began to warm the dew on the ground. Slowly, the dew retreated back into the ground as it did each morning losing the battle with the sun. Ora had already risen before the sunrise to prepare a fire to cook breakfast. She had the eggs, bread, and potatoes on the metal stove. There was still coffee from the day before in the pot, and she thought to herself she could just warm it up and no one would know the difference. The light beamed through the window now and began to light the wall behind her. She still felt sore and tired. She took off her apron and walked up to the door, opened it, and walked outside.

There was a hill with three trees on it out away from the house. It was just past the wood on the northern part of their property. She walked out to the hill and leaned on the tree. The sunlight hit her on the back as she looked to the west. There she saw the valley, hills, and farms of the neighboring counties that would lead down to the river. It was in these moments where silence and thought calmed her and overtook her. She knew that she was insignificant in the world. She would think of San Francisco, New York, and Philadelphia where buildings and streets were lined with people. She had been to Cincinnati before, and loved the city, but felt called beyond its booming streets and architecture. She felt pulled to a reality that was different from her own, in this part of Ohio, but felt that it would forever be out of her grasp.

She thought of her parents, especially her mother. Suddenly the silence broke. She heard him calling out for her from the house. It was like thunder cutting through the silence of a peaceful night. His voice carried through the trees. She prayed to herself silently before walking back to the house.

"Ora, it is time for breakfast?" he bellowed. Nathaniel had started the fire on the stove but had left the house to go to the shack where the cow, hogs, and chicken were kept. It was not so much of a barn as a pen with shanty roof over one side. She closed the door and could him whistling to himself outside. The pan was warm, and she placed the butter inside of it. As it began to melt, she shifted the pan above the flame to spread the butter. She put the potatoes inside of it after she had cut them up. She then cracked the eggs and dropped them into the pan as well.

"That smells good," Nathaniel said to her as he came in to wash up.

"It's almost ready Mr. Worshrieber. How are the animals this morning?" she asked him.

"The hogs are fine. The cow still won't give us any milk," he said defeated.

The food was just about ready as she began to spoon the food onto a plate and placed it in front of Mr. Weber.

"Thank you," he said as he poured himself some coffee. He took a drink, and she held her breath as she stood at the stove waiting for his reaction. He didn't notice it was the safe as the day before, and she quietly exhaled to herself. She made a plate for herself and joined him at the table.

Before she could taste her breakfast, he asked, "Well, will the doctor pay you for last month?"

"I asked him yesterday, and he told me it would be another week. There was some medication he had owed a bill on." She lied to him knowing the truth would only upset him this morning.

"That man never pays you on time. Dammit, I need that money. With the way the harvest is looking and the cows, I will be short with Koch again. That bastard!"

She took a bite of her food while he continued to talk. "I will remind him later today." She bit her tongue, and the tension ate at her. He didn't used to be this way before.

"We are three month's late on payments to him. He is threatening to take the plot from me. Tell him we need him to pay you!"

"I will Mr. Worshrieber," she said in total agreement. She did not want to upset him. Her arm was sore from where he hit her the day before.

"I am going to try and sell the cow today at the market and get what I can for her. I know you help as much as you can, and you work, but have you thought more about what we talked about? About working in town at the saloon?"

"You mean the brothel?" she said as tears welled up in her eyes. She saw that he was pouring himself a bit of whiskey as he stood behind her near the shelves. It was only half past eight in the morning.

"It would only be for a while to help me make right with him. Then you can stop. You're a pretty girl Ora and would only need a month or two before we are square."

"That is an awful thing to say to someone, to tell someone to do something like that. All I have done is help as much as I could since you took us on," she replied with tears.

"I have been caring for you since your mother passed some five years ago after your dad died. You owe me something for that. Feeding you and your sister, putting a roof over your head. Helping bury your momma after she got sick with the typhoid. You owe me that much, or I got to put you out on the street."

"I've been contributing the whole time. I cook and clean, work at the doc, and now you are asking me to be a powder girl to help pay your debt from gambling away your money," she said in between her sobbing.

He stood up and grabbed her by the shoulders and slapped her.

"Don't go making me feel guilty for anything! You can leave whenever you want!" he shouted. He slapped her face with the back of his hand. The mark began to turn red.

As soon as he let go of her, she grabbed her face and began sobbing. She fell back in the chair and continued crying. He kept screaming over her, that she was to go inquire about the payment and job at the saloon right away. He left the house and slammed the door behind him. She sat there and tried to wipe her tears on the drying cloth she had stuffed into her apron. It took a few minutes for her to gather herself before she stood up. She breathed deeply and straightened her blouse. She turned to the table and began clearing the dishes. She placed them in the empty washing bucket.

At this moment the horse neighed as he dug his spurs in to take off. She looked out through the window and saw them riding off toward the Montier's homestead that was just two miles to the south across the prairie. Most likely to work for some whiskey or drink with the old man Davey. She didn't feel disappointed he left, but relief. She cleaned up what was left of the breakfast and walked outside to feed it to the hogs. They looked sickly, and that is hard thing to do for a pig.

She walked outside to the well for some water. She pumped four buckets and filled the washing station. Before she cleaned the dishes, she washed her face and dried the tears. She began to wash the dishes, and after a few minutes, began to calm down. The morning still began to warm and soon with the peace and quiet, she would have some time to herself. She dried the last dish and poured herself from water into a glass from their well water jug in the kitchen and walked outside. She sat on the chair and relaxed for a few minutes.

She had not told him the doctor hadn't been paying her because he was leaving town. He needed to go be with his family in Philadelphia as his mother was ill and would need to attend to her estate. He only owed her the wages for the previous month and that would not be enough. He had been a good boss to her, and she looked forward to arriving into his office each time she had to work. He showed her how to do bookkeeping and write paperwork for patients over the last year. His practice began to take off because he could visit his patients in their homes more with Ora helping with the bookkeeping. She enjoyed it and even would read the medical books that lined his shelves. On slow days, she would try pronouncing the Latin words in the book. She knew French and this helped her, but she often had to be corrected.

Her mother was French and would speak French to her. Most folks in these parts spoke German, so her ability was a rarity. Ora would sing the songs and church hymns in French since her mother's passing to herself. Her sister would not speak it often as she had begun to take on the speech patterns of their neighbors, a mix of frontier English and German pronunciation. In many ways, her sister had forgotten their past and could just adapt to a new situation with ease. It was not that way for Ora. She always had to fight with change. Ora felt it was why she clung to French as a way to keep her mother close in her heart since the typhoid. Here she was lost in thoughts again when her sister finally arrived home.

"Morning Ora," Loren said to her as she pulled the carriage up to the porch. She got off the carriage and tied the reins to the wood horse ledge. She walked up to her and gave her a hug.

"It is good to see you."

Ora replied, "It is good to see you too. I haven't seen you at home much this week."

"Samuel and I have just had a wonderful time together. We went swimmin' and walkin' through the hills. I helped him in the kitchen and with the animals. We went into town one of the days too. His family makes pretty good dandelion wine. We were sitting one night, and he made me laugh so hard that I spit out my wine into his face."

Ora laughed out loud. They kept talking, and Ora felt so happy for her sister. She had been glowing since becoming so close with Samuel several months earlier. He was a short man, but thick in the shoulders. He had brown hair and green eyes. He treated her well enough and had made an effort to get to know her very well. He provided the stability for her sister that she needed. More than that he was a way out. This made Ora so happy for her because she did not want her to deal with the verbal and physical abuse.

"I am so happy for you Loren," Ora said to her.

"Thank you. I hope you don't feel I have been selfish by not being here to help support you."

Ora replied, "I just want what is best for you. You are younger than me and shouldn't be around him Nathaniel. It is alright."

"You won't have to worry about that, He asked me to marry him." She interjected He purchased and received a land deed out in Colorado about six or seven weeks ago like I told you. He wants to leave soon to beat the winter on the way out there."

Loren kept talking, and Ora just said she was so happy for her and the opportunity it would provide the two of them.

"I am so happy for you," she said. They both hugged. "It will be wonderful in Colorado. Where will his plot be?"

"It will be south of Denver, so we will be in the mountains. It will be cold in the winters, but beautiful. I think we are about two weeks away from leaving. I wanted to ask you, would you like to come with? I need you to leave this place."

Her question surprised her, and it was a relief to picture a future from what this had become. She felt the wind on her face and looked into her sister's eyes, "I didn't think you would ask me. Of course, I will come with and I won't be a burden. I swear!"

"You won't be a burden for us at all. It will be wonderful. There is one thing though, the fare is $30 dollars for food and to help support us when we get there. I have raised $10, and Thomas has produced the rest for me from his wages. You have some money stashed away hidden in the house, right? You have that much in there, right? We don't have any other money to pay for the extra travel fair with the party."

"I have $23, and Doctor Weber will be paying me this week before he leaves for Philadelphia. I should have enough from that, and I can sell a few things around the house to get close to that." Ora sounded so excited in her voice. They sat drinking tea and laughed on the porch and laughed for a few hours as they shared stories from their youth.

"You look tired Ora? What is wrong?" Loren asked her when their laughter subsided. She leaned in and put her hand on Ora's knee. She looked at her concerned.

"He is months behind paying the loan on this place and says that they will be taking the plot back. His drinking has been getting worse, and he gets mean when he is drinking." She stopped keeping the tears back. "I enjoy working at the Doctor's so much and have learned so much, but he is leaving too. I just have to get away from here."

Loren hugged her and held her close. They both cried together. "We will both have a new life soon. A new beginning." Loren made a joke about her future husband's endowment to lighten the mood, and they both laughed.

They stood up and walked from the porch over to the carriage. They untied the horses from the hitching rail. They checked the reins as well to make sure all was well.

"I have to be going now but will be back in two weeks to get you. I love you and will see you soon." Loren told her before she got onto the carriage.

Ora replied back, "I love you too and will be counting the days." She waved to her and stood watching as Loren rode off into the distance.

It was just past noon based on where the sun was in the sky. She went into the stable and brushed her horse, Maple. She named her this several years before because she was sweet like syrup. She went and grabbed her saddle from the house and threw it over Maple's back. She grabbed her old worn brown hat and got up on her horse. She rode him through the gate and out to the road towards the doctor' place.

It was a several mile journey. It should only take an hour she thought. The trees and breeze felt so good on her face as the day had warmed. She felt some sweat on her brow, which rolled down from her forehead and off her nose. As she got to the large oak tree at the front of the doctor's lawn, she slowed Maple down by pulling on the reins.

The doctor's house was a faded blue with black shutters. He had an addition added to the side of the house where the patients would be examined, and any surgeries would be performed. These were usually minor if they occurred at all. She put her horse in the stable and set her saddle in the barn. She ran inside and greeted the doctor. He had just finished with Mrs. Morkle as she was walking out of the patient room. She said hello to Ora.

"You look nice today Ora." She said.

"So do you Mrs. Morkle, and I hope the doctor has you feeling better." Ora said with a smile.

"He has me on the mend," she replied. She walked with a limp. Mrs. Morkle was a woman in her late fifties and saw her health begin to decline greatly. She walked from the doctor's house the two hundred yards or so back into town where her husband was working at the mill.

"So great to hear that," Ora said

"Hello doctor. How are you today?" she asked him.

He was reading some notes on her and then was comparing them to a book he had taken off the shelf. He was giving her an elixir to ease her stomach pain but the pain had been getting worse.

"I am concerned for Mrs. Morkle. Her pain is around her liver and is starting to affect her appetite. After going through the journals, I suspect it is cancer now but can't be sure. I told her today it could be and recommended she see my friend in Dayton after I leave next week. She will likely die of cancer in the next year and a half, probably sooner," he said with great concern. Ora's heart sunk from hearing the news.

"What was your question, oh right. Yes, my day is good. Now, I have the wages I owe you. There is something extra for all your work as well." He had walked into his office which was now covered in boxes and crates that were still empty and not packed. He found an envelope with her name on it. A smile came on his face, and he turned toward her. "Here you are. I am definitely going to miss having you work with me. You would make a great doctor or nurse one day."

Ora smiled at him and looked up at him. He had been a father figure to her these past three years. She gave him a hug. "Thank you for everything. I can't tell you what it meant to me to learn from you. When will you be leaving?"

"You're welcome. I am leaving in two days. The carriage from the company I hired will be here tomorrow. I will ride to Cleveland and then take the train east to Philadelphia. It should be a five-day journey. I will write to you when I get there. Now get out of here and get out of this town before it consumes you," he said with a smile. Like all their conversations, it had been kept brief, punctual, but sincere. He always described his struggles relating to people to her and she understood why he stayed reserved and clinical. She felt thankful he had strayed from this during their goodbye.

She hugged him one more time and then turned and walked back outside. She put the envelope in her saddle bag. She petted the horse's face until he voiced his approval. She jumped up on the saddle and rode toward the town. She headed onto the main street and tied her horse outside the main store. She picked her dress up so she didn't trip on the steps and went into the store.

She said hello to the shop clerk Homer. He waved to her from behind the counter while he looked through the new inventory that had just arrived. She went through the aisles and picked out the items she wished to purchase. She kept staring at which type of soap she wanted to purchase as they had a new type that smelled like lavender. She thought to herself that it would be worth having this one indulgence. She walked up to the counter and placed the bag of grain, flour, soap, potatoes, and carrots onto the counter. He began to calculate the cost and got to the soap and stopped.

"This is the expensive French soap. It costs $.25," Homer asked her with surprise.

"I know, I thought I would spoil myself for a change Homer."

Homer smiled, "Good, you deserve it dear. That will be $.75."

Ora laid out the coins on the counter and then got the items back in a sack from Homer. They exchanged goodbyes, and she went walked back to Maple. The street was very busy with traffic. Several large wagons were down the street dropping off lumber at the mill. She stopped and stared toward the saloon. She could see the girls inside with their dresses. It was three stories tall that had been painted a dark red on the outside with black trim. She stared so long that one of the girls made eye contact with her through the window. In that second, she felt such relief that she wouldn't have to resort to this with the money she had just been paid by the doctor.

She put the items onto the back of her horse and closed the rear sack. She untied Maple from the post and then pulled herself up onto the saddle. She turned the horse around and looked back to the saloon one more time. The light flickered into her eye off the window, and she had to squint. A large group of men passed in front of her and whistled. They each walked into the saloon as the doors swung open. The hinges needed to be replaced she thought to herself.

Finally, she was headed back to her home. Soon the bustle of town had faded into the distance as she rode along the creek. The water flowing made a soothing sound that you could hear if you focused in hard enough. The flowers were in bloom and tall all along both sides of the trail. The butterflies and bees crisscrossed in such a way that they were almost like fireflies at night, she thought. The willow trees branches made the trail up ahead very dense so she always took this slow to not startle Maple.

After a mile or so of following the creek, she reached the field that led to their house. It opened to the field, and she pushed the horse as fast as it would go. Her hair was shooting straight behind her head it seemed as she stood talk in the reins. She then sat back down in the saddle and had the horse trot around the hill up to the cabin. She was in such a wonderful mood. Singing songs and thinking to herself how beautiful her new life was going to be.

Finally, she reached the cabin and rode Maple up to the fence and dismounted. She took the reins and walked her inside the wood fence. She closed the gate and walked back over to her. She took the saddle off slowly and then placed it on the top beam of the fence. She went back and brushes the hair on Maple's back to prevent a rash from forming. The sun fell in the sky as it started to set. The red and orange hue cut through the sky and illuminated the clouds. She was brushing the horses back as it had its head down eating grain. Suddenly she noticed that he was not home, and the other his horse was gone.

She set down the brush and slipped in between the beams of the fence and walked over to the house.

"Hello, is anyone here?" she asked with alarm.

No one replied for several seconds, and she asked again. She went back to the saddle and opened the pouch. She took the sack of goods and the envelope full of money. She turned toward the house and walked into the kitchen. She called again, and there was no reply. She felt confident that she was alone. She put away the goods from the store in kitchen and then knew now was the time to go to her room which was in the rear behind the kitchen down the hallway. It was dark enough inside her room that she needed to light a lamp. She opened the drawer next to the stove on her right and took out a match. She used it to light the oil lamp in her room. She put the money she had into the secret nook under her bed. She put the block back to secure it and got up off the floor. The room was still poorly lit, and she stood up. She took the lamp and now opened the drawer and lit a match to light the oil lamp sitting on the kitchen table.

She walked back to her room and opened the door. The hinges creaked as the door swung open. She paused to make sure she heard no other noises. She held up the lamp to illuminate the room. She moved the lamp to the right and then to left. She did not see anyone or anything suspicious. She took a step in and felt her toe hit something as she kicked it across the floor. She kneeled while holding the lamp out and screamed, "No!!!"

It was the piece of wood from her bed frame where she had been hiding her money she had been saving. She fell to the ground and set the lamp on the floor and search frantically under the bed. She found the open sack she kept her money in the back corner under her bed. He tossed it in plain sight after he grabbed the money she thought.

She buried her head into her bed crying. "It's gone!" she screamed. She had no way to leave with her sister now. She punched her mattress with her fists until they were started to bruise. She didn't care about the pain in her knuckles. It was just one more memory that would fade away. She lay on the floor for a long time. She continued to cry until she fell asleep.

Before she fell asleep for good, she kept thinking to herself the only way to make that money would be to work at the brothel. She kept sobbing to herself thinking she may be able to make enough money in the next two weeks to where they would let her go, even if she was short a few dollars. The air grew cold. She finally stood up from the floor and then fell onto her bed. Suddenly, the light went out as the last bit of oil burned out in the lamp. She stared into nothing. She felt nothing.

***

The morning came slowly. The light came through the window and pierced her eyes. Ora blinked as it stung her eyes, and she raised her hand up to block the light from hurting her eyes until they adjusted. She rolled onto her back. It didn't take long before her mind began racing again. She wanted to believe it was all a dream. She pushed herself up out of bed and looked into the mirror in front of her. Her eyes were swollen from the tears. She looked down and noticed how dusty her dress was near her feet. She shook her dress with her hands and then patted it to dust it some more.

She looked into the mirror. Her hair was tangled, and none of it agreed with the other. She pulled her hair back and used pins to hold it up in place. She walked out into the kitchen and took some water to wash her face. She took an apple she had purchase the day before and took a bite. She tapped her fingers on table rapidly. She stared out for a period of time into nothing. She dropped the apple core and went back into her room. She took the money out of the sack the doctor paid her the day before and put it in her pocket.

She walked outside toward the stable. She grabbed the saddle that sat on the fence and walked over to the gate and opened it. The hinges on that creaked loudly. It was almost rusted through. Maple seemed excited to see her. She took the saddle over and threw it over the horse. She petted the animal with her hand before she threw her first foot up into the reins before she threw her other leg over the horse, but it caught its back so she leaned forward to not fall off.

"Shit!" she cried out before finding her balance. She pulled the reins tight to the left, and the horse turned with her. Her knuckles went white when she squeezed the reins. Her hands still hurt from the night before. She shook her hand and tried to laugh off her gaffe. The horse nickered as it turned its head toward her. It was as if the animal itself felt her distress and wanted to say it is okay. She leaned forward and put her cheek on the horse's neck and ran her hand up its neck.

"Thanks," she said as she kept petting her neck. "Let's go girl."

They tore off as she pulled on the reins. The horse seemed to move faster and faster with each step. The trees and scenery moved past them like a blur. It felt like a dream and they slowed when they saw the outskirts of town. All she could remember was the creek and the open meadow, nothing else. It was then that the people walking across the street seemed like they were moving through thigh deep mud. She felt like mosquitoes were biting her neck. She was breathing heavy and felt a panic as her chest felt like it was tightening. "Just breathe," she kept telling herself.

The townsfolk paid her no attention, and she continued down to the stable. She dismounted and paid the manager the fee of five cents for keeping her horse for the day. It was hard for her to not allow her shoulders to slouch as she felt defeated inside. The street was mostly empty, and her vision focused solely on the building ahead. Everything else became blocked out. She walked over to the saloon but stopped on the first step. Her feet did not want to move, and she felt as if a mountain was pushing her slowly into the dirt. She looked in the through the doors and picked up her first foot.

The board creaked under her foot as she stepped onto the boardwalk under the porch. She took another step until she pushed open the door in front of her. It creaked as it swung open. The room smelled of tobacco, townsfolk, and incense that hung in the air to cover the stale smell of sweat and dirt. It had a hint of lilac and some vanilla in it. The woman she had seen the day before looked at her from across the room with beady eyes. It was a look of contempt and joy, as this girl took pleasure in Ora's apprehension. The swing door still creaked as it had not stopped swinging behind her because the spring had been over tightened.

The Madame walked over to Ora and extended her hand.

"Hello my dear. What brings you to our fine establishment this morning?" Madame Porcella asked her. As she said this, she took Ora's hand as if she was reading her mind and walked her over to the bar. "Travis, I think she could use some sweet brandy. Bring me two glasses."

Travis did not reply or move his head. While looking down, he merely placed two glasses on the oak wood bar top and then filled each with brandy out of a dusty old glass bottle. Madame Porcella thanked Travis, who now looked up and met her gaze. He had a glass eye and a scar extending up from the same socket. The woman handed the glass to Ora and looked at her. Ora smelled the liquor before she took a drink. It smelled delicious and expensive to her. Ora opened her mouth to speak, but the woman stopped her.

"First drink, then we will talk," she said back to Ora.

Each took the brandy down slowly and placed the glass back onto the oak bar top. The music continued to play from the piano in the corner. It was a sonata from a lesser European composer. The notes matched the apprehension Ora felt in her heart. The morning was still early, but the patrons were talking loudly across the room. Ora waited for Madame to speak and looking at her she noticed the rugs on the floor behind her. The rugs added an elegance that was heightened by the English style wallpaper and glass chandeliers above their heads.

"Now, I have seen you look at this place with disdain in your eyes as you walk by us in the street. You judge me and everyone in here. The question I have for you, is what brings you here to sit with me and have brandy, heaven forbid before noon for a self-righteous girl such as yourself?"

Ora tried to speak but couldn't find the words at first as she looked at the floor and then looked back to her. The woman took her hand and squeezed it firmly.

"My dear, there is no judgment here. Necessity causes us to take actions we never thought we would."

Ora felt cold, but Madame's hand felt warm. This made her feel more reassured with herself to speak.

"I want to work for you and I need the money, and there is no other way I can save up enough to leave town with my sister." She felt so ashamed and her face turned red. The music kept playing, but the room began to spin.

The woman panted her hand. "No, you don't want to work for me. I have heard that before. You need to work for me. The funny thing is we all say the same thing, and the truth is . . . We never do get to leave. So, what is it that you think we do here?"

"You sleep with men for money," she replied despondently. Her face was plain, her hair tucked back other than a few strands that fell forward on her face. She brushed it back. The smell of lilac returned. She couldn't notice the vanilla.

"No, no dear," she said shaking her head. "That is a whore house. Yes, we sleep with men on occasion . . . for the right price, but we make our money on the experience." Madame shifted her weight and then pointed to the room. "Most everyone wants to be something else, to feel more important than they actually are. We let the sad saps that walk in those doors to forget about their poor existence for a few hours. That is what we do here. Sex is such a small part of it."

"Oh, I didn't think of it that way," Ora replied, trying to hide the contempt and sarcasm in her voice. The sun light reflecting off the glass caused her to squint. She thought she could manage by just playing a part.

"Listen Ora," the lady cut her off. "I need to know if you are comfortable doing that if you want to work here. You are beautiful, and we need a new blood in here to satisfy our customers. They have been fancying a new girl around here for a while. Are you willing to play a part? If you can, you may just be able to leave."

Madame leaned closer and let her words sink in deeply. She had intentionally faced away from the windows to have Ora's eyes blinded. Ora couldn't see the greed in her eyes.

Ora paused and felt her stomach turn over as she knew she had to agree. The vomit rose to the back of her throat. She held it down and said calmly, "I can do that for you," Ora lied and hid her hand shaking. She hated herself in that moment. She thought she might faint as she felt a part of herself die.

"Precisely. Now, can you be back here all dolled up two days from now at 7:30 in the evening. I think it is best if you jump right in, and we will see if you can act as well as you speak."

"Alright, I will see you at half past seven."

Ora stood up and the woman finally let go of her hand. She turned and walked toward the door.

"Oh, and dear, please make sure to wear something a little more flattering than what you have on."

"I will. The best I have," she said and walked out into the street. Her heart sank, and she felt numb. She turned back to the girl in the far corner of the room. She still wore a devilish smile on her face. It cut right through her. All Ora could do was look away and leave the saloon. Her head held high, but she held back tears. She did her best to rationalize that this would lead to greater things as she rode the horse back home.

Chapter 5

Two days later, Ora finally made it to the saloon. It had taken her this long to rationalize and gather the courage to do this. They had music playing on the piano. The notes seemed to cut through the heavy smoke to the reach ceiling and reverberate back to the floor. The air smelled of cigarettes as the patrons were smoking but the saloon owner would put out potpourri to cut the smell. It did the job well as the air had cooled because of a storm front coming in. Ora wiped some sweat from her brow with a handkerchief and stood at the corner of the bar looking around and tapped her leg with her finger nervously. She glanced past the bartender and looked at herself in the mirror. Her eyes seemed a darker shade than normal, and it was the first time she was truly disgusted with herself that she could remember. Her inner voice kept screaming at her, but she refused to listen.

"Ora, dear, you aren't here to be a decoration on the wall. Go make friends with some of the fine gentlemen. Relax, go have fun," Madame Porcella said.

"I'm sorry Madame Porcella. I am just nervous."

Fun she thought to herself, she has to be kidding.

"The sooner you get the first one over with, the easier it gets. Just think about something else," she said and pushed Ora out toward the gaming tables.

Ora felt flush and began to walk up and speak to the patrons. She had worn the only nice garment she owned, a royal blue dress. Her future depended on a few short weeks of this she kept repeating to herself. The men had missing teeth, dirt on their trousers, or shirts that hadn't been washed or pressed for some time. Some wore nice suits and appeared to be business men. She hoped for one of the business men, if it had to happen at all.

Outside the bar, Everett Gunn arrived in the town after a three days ride. They had finished a simple job after the first one and then he rode off towards Cincinnati. He had not taken a boat ferry in some time to cross the Mississippi. The drought had lowered the water from the banks. His backside hurt from riding, and he had barely eaten in three days. He grimaced from the discomfort that ran from his back and hip down to his left foot. He found the stable and rode down to it paying no attention to the patrons on the street. When he reached the stable, he got off his horse. He took the saddle bags off the horse and took his rifle out of the holster. The stable boy came over to greet him. Gunn reached into his pocket and paid the boy to place his horse in the stable.

He took his rifle with his one hand and pulled his saddle bags with his other and walked back out into the street. The wind felt like a knife cutting through him as the jacket pushed against his back. He looked up to the sky and saw nothing but black clouds. He carried the rifle in his right hand to balance out the slight limp from his left hip. He looked down the street and saw the saloon. He thought to himself that this was his best bet to stay warm. He sighed aloud as he shivered. The money felt heavy in his pocket. He wanted to sleep in a warm bed and find the bath house in the morning.

As he took a few more steps, he looked to his right into the window of the store and saw the goods on the shelf behind the counter. There were several types of candies, each different type of candy that seemed sweeter than the last. He felt into his pocket for paper and tobacco. His fingers fidgeted but felt no tobacco inside the pocket. He stepped up onto the wood planks and then into store. The step was uneven and slanted toward the front. The floorboards showed cracks halfway through the board. He pushed open the door with his left hand. The store smelled of grain and stale items. The clerk greeted him and asked him to leave his rifle by the door. The store clerk looked tense seeing Gunn standing there with a rifle.

"Just here for tobacco friend," Gunn said.

Everett looked at him and kept walking over to the shelves that had rolling paper and tobacco. The limp ever so noticeable. The clerk relaxed his face and shoulders after this. Gunn knelt down to read the types of tobacco. There were three types. Everett picked up a bit of each and smelled it. He rolled the leaves in his left hand between his fingers. He found one he liked and put some in the small pouch.

He decided to buy some cartridges as well. He surveyed the remaining items for several minutes as his body warmed. As his feet moved across the floor boards, each one creaked or shifted a little. He looked through the window of the store and saw the saloon across the street. He thought that a warm drink would do nicely. Through the window, he saw a woman in a blue dress. She had brown hair but seemed reserved and uncomfortable as some of the men talked to her. Something looked out of place he thought.

The thunder had just started, the sky lit up from the lighting. The flashes came through the window. The rain began to pour and pounded the roof overhead. Gunn gingerly walked up to the counter.

"Box of long cartridges," Gunn said. The clerk turned and walked to his left and selected the box for the rifle and held it up. Gunn nodded to him. The clerk turned back and placed it on the counter. He rang up the total, and Gunn put the money on the counter to purchase the North Carolina tobacco, rolling papers, and cartridges. The clerk handed him his change, and he put his billfold back in his jackets internal pocket on the left side. He thanked the clerk and exited the store.

He stopped under the awning and rolled a cigarette. He took his time as the rain had picked up and became heavier. He lit the match and enjoyed a long drag. No sense in not enjoying a cigarette before getting wet he thought. The rain sounded like pings as the droplets hit the tin shingles on some of the nearby buildings. By the time he finished, the street had started to become a swamp from the rain. It was not too deep, but it was slick. This aggravated his back more as the dirt turned mud. He had to pull and twist his feet to get them out with each step. As he reached the boardwalk and porch, he kicked the mud off his boots.

He pushed the door open and exclaimed, "Like crossing the damn Ohio," to the girl in the purple dress who greeted everyone next to the door as she looked down at his feet and the rain falling off his jacket onto the floor. She smiled at him and laughed, and he tipped his cap.

"Do you have a storage room?" he asked her.

"We do, it is down the hall on the right."

"Thanks, miss," Gunn said.

He walked over to the hall and found the room. The man behind the counter took his rifle and saddle bags. He locked them in a locker and gave Gunn a token. Neither man said anything heartfelt to the other. Gunn walked back to the main area with just his pistols, wallet, and his jacket. He beat the water droplets off of it before he went inside.

He made his way over to the bar, working his way through the crowd until found an opening between two different men. He walked up and filled the space. He leaned his hip against the bar. He straightened his back. He raised his hand to get the bartender's attention. The bartender raised his hand with two fingers, as if to say I will be there in two minutes. Gunn looked back and then turned his head toward the organ. The man sitting there played a tune with real swing. The gaming tables had lots of action on them, and the sound from the roulette wheel carried through the crowd. Some of the players had intense focus as their money rode the line. They didn't speak a word. There were men in dark suits at the black jack table. These patrons were loud, joyful, and paid no attention to the rain outside. He looked around for the woman in the blue dress he had seen through the window. She was to his right as he faced the gaming tables, two men down from him.

Ora squinted her eyes in the corner of her eyes from the disgust and stress of going through with this charade. She did it with laughter at all the terrible jokes and stories. She wore her hair up and used hair pins to hold it in place. Several men had tried talking with her throughout the night. Each was more revolting than the last. The current man claimed to be a cowboy up from Tennessee and that he knew Davey Crockett for a time. He seemed much too young to have known Crockett, especially since he died at the Alamo many years prior.

The cowboy kept rambling about the herd master screwing him out of his share of the money. She kept eye contact and smiled as best she could to look interested, but every opportunity he took to break the touch barrier she recoiled. The kind of half-hearted smile you give a friend that thinks they are a closer friend than they really are. They all bored her and terrified her.

Ora stood to Gunn's left as he faced away from the bar. She noticed the side of his face and tilted her head for a moment to focus on him. She crunched her brow and studied him for a few seconds.

"Are you alright?" a man asked her.

"Oh yes, I am sorry. I just feel warm," she replied before taking a drink.

"Happens to women when they talk to me," the man said back.

She laughed to herself in her head but forced herself to say back, "We will have to see." She almost threw up in her mouth but kept the whiskey down. He went back into conversing and ordered another round.

Finally, the bartender came back and tapped Gunn on the shoulder. "What'll it be?" he asked before Gunn could turn around.

Gunn turned back toward the bartender and saw Ora standing past the man to his right. Another man stood there vying for her attention. Her blue dress made her stand out from the people around her. She still looked uncomfortable, but her eyes met his for a second. He thought to himself that she seemed out of place in a place this and seemed tense. He held his gaze until she looked away. He moved the man next to him out of the way as he got closer to her.

The bartender waited until after Gunn moved to repeat himself.

"So, what'll it be?" the bartender repeated

"Brandy."

He looked at the bartender briefly and then returned his focus to Ora. He noticed the outline of her face as she talked.

The bartender replied, "The brandy is not due in for another week. We have rye and corn whiskey, also have moonshine." He raised the bottle waiting for Gunn's approval. Gunn pointed to the moonshine. Whatever the hell will warm me up he thought. The bartender poured Gunn's moonshine in a clean glass and started a tab for him. Gunn took the glass and raised it to his mouth to take a drink. It felt good going down his throat and warmed him. He turned away from the bartender and glanced at Ora again in reflection in the mirror. He then looked back across the room. He took a few moments to decide if he should play cards or order some food and go to bed. He had enough money in his pocket and could do it all if he wanted. He felt eager to do something with it. He finished his drink and pointed to the bartender for another. He filled the glass, and Gunn took it. He saw the tables were full, and the crowd didn't seem to be the kind that would make good company. He decided he wouldn't try his luck at the games tonight.

A woman in a pink and black dress walked up to him.

"Looks like you didn't beat the storm."

Gunn turned to her and looked down as she was half a foot shorter than he him. Gunn's jacket still had rain droplets on it. He had tucked the jacket behind the long barrel pistol on his right hip and the handle of the gun was pointed toward her.

"Didn't quite make it," he replied.

"I have not seen you around here before. Are you new to town?" she asked as she moved closer and touched the handle of the gun on his hip. She looked up at him with her green eyes.

"Just passing through."

He looked to his right and caught the Ora's eyes again. She looked at him and then looked away. He gave her no expression as he looked at her. The cowboy was still talking to her, and she turned her attention back to him. He had placed his hand on the small of her back and had begun soliciting her for some of her time. This establishment was a brothel after all. The cowboy's actions irritated him for some reason.

The women in the pink dress said to him, "She is already spoken for. If you are looking for a good time, why don't you and I go upstairs and get to know each other?" She put her hand on his hip.

"Appreciate it miss. Not interested."

"Special price, we can negotiate," she said back.

"Appreciate it miss. Price ain't the issue."

He looked at her and turned back toward the bar. Ora had listened to his exchange and glanced at him. She thought he looked dignified despite looking rough. He took the glass and finished the remaining moonshine in his glass. The woman walked away from him quite annoyed. She was not used to bar patrons saying no to her. He got the bartender's attention and pointed to his glass for the another shot. The bartender uncorked the same bottle and poured more into his glass.

"Most men don't turn her down," he said. "She has regulars."

"She won't miss my business then. Do you have any open rooms for the evening?" Gunn asked.

"Just the one suite left. It'll be a dollar a night," the bartender said to him.

"I need it for the night. Have some food brought up in an hour," Gunn said.

"We have some roast and potatoes," the bartender replied.

Everett said that would be just fine and laid the money on the bar. The bartender had his helper go and fetch the key from the desk. He took the money and gave the key to Everett.

"There is water in the pitcher for washing. And soap on the dresser. Bottle of wine in there too."

"Thank you," Everett said.

He thought of the bed and warm food. He turned to walk up the stairs and saw the cowboy speaking with Ora. He was pulling her towards him and trying to kiss her cheek. She was resisting him still. He began insulting her because of her rejection. He grew madder and madder as his face turned a dark red. Again, Gunn thought it peculiar a woman in a brothel was insistent on not becoming friendly with a customer. He felt drawn to her, similar to the call towards violence he felt with his revolvers. The man grabbed her posterior and called her a whore. She slapped his hand away and said to him, "Va te faire foute."

Everett understood her cursing this man out in French. Telling him to go fuck himself. He decided to wait and listen to their conversation. It was like one of those comedy plays he had wanted to see as a child. He studied the tension in her face and the eagerness in the cowboy's.

"Ooh a French-speaking lady. French ladies are supposed to enjoy this sort of thing," he said to her.

Madame Porcella noticed this as she walked over. She addressed the situation and apologized to the man by taking his hand. She tried to redirect his anger away from Ora. He turned and called Ora a whore again.

Madame Porcella turned and began verbally beating Ora with words.

"I will give her to you for free."

Ora felt anxious and couldn't make any words and was doing her best to not cry. A white heat crept up Gunn's spine like a spider on a wall until it stopped behind his eyes. At this moment, Everett had enough and stepped over to the three of them.

"You best apologize to the lady," Gunn exclaimed to the cowboy as Madame Porcella stood talking to the cowboy. Both turned and looked at Gunn with raised eyes and mouths agape. He stood the same size as Gunn but looked meaner and rougher.

"Mind your business, I'll speak to the whore how I want," he said back to him.

Ora's eyes went wide and blinked once at Gunn. She stood frozen and couldn't move. As the man shouted back at him, Gunn repeated himself, "I said you best apologize to the lady."

The cowboy replied, "Lady, you mean whore."

Gunn took his right hand and had lowered it to his holster as they spoke and tucked his jacket behind the revolver. The man moved closer to Gunn to confront him as he did this. Gunn drew the pistol and struck the man right on the forehead with it. This knocked him back two steps as blood ran down his forehead from an open gash. Gunn stepped toward him as he staggered back and hit him over the head with the butt of his gun again. This dropped the cowboy to the floor. Gunn cocked the pistol and pointed it at his face.

Madame Porcella backed away toward the center of the room. Ora, whose back was against the bar and couldn't move, stood in shock as Gunn beat this man. The patrons cleared away to make a circle around them. The dazed and bloodied cowboy cried out not to be shot. Water droplets dripped off the bottom of his jacket onto the floor as he said don't kill me. Gunn stared through the cowboy and pierced the soul of his man.

The bartender screamed, "Enough. Not in my establishment! Don't you pull that trigger." He pointed a shotgun at Everett with both barrels cocked.

Gunn turned and looked at bartender and turned back to the man. He held the gun out, ready to shoot, and widened his eyes at the cowboy. Daring him to try anything other than what Gunn had said.

The cowboy, through the blood coming down his forehead, turned and apologized to Ora. "I am sorry miss," he muttered.

Gunn uncocked his pistol and put it back in his holster. Slowly, the tension of the situation settled down, and each of the bar patrons evaporated away like morning dew. The music started playing again, and the patrons started gambling again (sometimes, a little swing music goes a long way). Within moments, it was as if nothing had happened. Other patrons helped the man to his feet and offered him a free beer. He demanded some whiskey, and the bartender obliged. They gave him a rag to wipe the blood off his forehead.

The woman in pink dress went over to him immediately, feeling this was her opportunity to make some money. Madame Porcella said his drinks were on the house for the evening and pointed to a different bottle of whiskey. She took it from the bartender and handed it over to him to enjoy after he finished the free shot. It was the bottle they had watered down earlier that day. Poor bastard would never know the different Madame Porcella thought to herself.

While all that was happening, Gunn turned back to the bar, and Ora looked at him.

"Thank you, sir." She waited for his reply.

He paused and studied her face. He said, "Je vous en prie."

The words caught her by surprise, but she understood them immediately. She stepped closer to him. He did not move, so she continued walking up to him. She was too shocked to speak. He moved past her towards the bar and took the key to his room off the top of the bar. Everyone moved to give him plenty of room as he walked by, and he took Ora's hand as he carried the key in his other hand.

As they moved through the crowd, Madame Porcella then walked up and scolded Ora by threatening to fire her. Ora's eyes teared up from frustration and embarrassment. Her face turned red, and she was blinking to hold back the tears. The heat crept up his neck again.

"You're not gonna do that," he said to her. He reached into his pocket and pulled out ten dollars. He put it in her hand. "Get that man a better bottle of whiskey too," he said as he pointed to the man he had just beaten senseless a few moments before. He leaned in and whispered to Madame Porcella's ear, "The one you didn't water down."

Madame Porcella stood wide eyed and embarrassed. She looked at him eyes as she was shocked he knew the trick.

Ora couldn't find the words and just continued to stand there. Gunn turned back to Ora. "Do you want something to eat?" he asked her in French. She turned and looked at him trying to focus on him. She tried to read him and determine his intentions.

"I would like that very much," she replied to him.

He looked back at the bartender and said to him. "Make that enough for two bar-keep."

The bartender nodded and added this to his room tab.

He turned back to Ora and said, "Follow me."

He grabbed her hand and led her to the stairs. She was scared and confused but could not resist him taking her hand and leading him up the stairs. She felt safer with him than with the chaos of the room below, almost as if she had found an ally. His hand did not harm her but held firm. After the bend in the staircase, she looked back to the patrons. They were all degenerates she thought. With each step she could hear his spurs and the sounds of the game room grew fainter. They reached the top of the stair case and turned into the hallway. His room was the last one all the way on the right. There was baroque-looking wall paper with a flower pattern on it. He let her hand go when they reached the floor. She kept following him and kept telling herself to breathe. The last remaining rain drops fell to the floor from his jacket.

Ora looked at the wood floor and studied the droplets. He reached the door and took the key and opened the door. With the door open, he stepped back and motioned with his hand to let her enter first. The hinges made a noise as the door swung open.

He entered the room after her and closed the door. The door had to be lifted slightly to align the lock, and after doing so, he locked it. She became frightened. All men wanted the same thing, but then she remembered he understood her speaking French. Still her fears became anxiety, and she went over next to the table to create as much space as she could from. She said him in English, "Thank you again for before."

"You're welcome," he replied in English.

"Parlez-vous Francais?" she inquired with her voice dropping as she finished her sentence. She stood their facing him. As if she was reading, she studied as she asked him as he locked the door. She had placed as much distance as she could between them.

"Oui," he said, "for a long time. Et toi?"

He was putting his hat on the dresser against the opposite from the door and ran his hand through his hair. He walked over and looked out the north and east windows. The rain was hammering down on the roof outside. As he inspected, there were no leaks. She stood and observed him until she worked up the courage to reply. She watched him before answering.

"My mother taught me," she said.

"Even the cuss words?" he asked as placed his hat on the dresser.

"Even the cuss words," she replied with a forced laugh. "Who taught you?"

"My mother did too," he said back to her calmly. They both nodded, and she sensed he was the telling the truth. She hoped he was. He hadn't made eye contact with her yet and rolled a cigarette. After he lit it, he took a drag and looked at her. The light from the oil lamp cast shadows across his face.

"What do you want from me?" she continued in French testing him, continuing to try and find even ground and balance.

He didn't answer. He took his jacket off and hung it up on the coat hook on the wall. He went over to the dresser and then poured water into the wash basin. He set his cigarette on the table and then washed his face and his hands in the cool water. She then sat on the chair waiting for him to answer. After he dried his face, he picked up the cigarette. The silence became uncomfortable. She repeated herself in English this time.

"That feels good," he said to her in French. "I haven't washed my face in three days." He exhaled and smoke left his mouth.

She felt uneasy as her question went unanswered so she repeated herself to him again.

He answered her in French, "You didn't look comfortable down there."

"You noticed that."

"The crinkle in the corner of your eye gave that away."

She paused and knew he was right. "I supposed it did. What do you want sir?" she asked him again.

"Conversation."

"Conversation, all you want is conversation," she repeated in English confused. She laughed to herself and put her hand over her mouth. She gathered herself and said, "I thought you wanted . . ."

"No. Not many French speaking folk in these parts. Especially, foul mouthed women like you," he said. He studied her at this moment and decided not to sit next to her. Her hair had a light brown color. She had slight freckles but tanned skin. He leaned back against the dresser and kept looking at her. He had almost finished his cigarette. She kept looking at it.

"Would you like one?" he asked her.

"No, thank you. Why did you help me and hit that man?" she asked softly. She could tell on how he leaned against the dresser he favored his left hip.

He switched back to French. "You don't belong with that filth downstairs. Clear as day."

"How do you know that?" she said to him.

"I just do," he said to her. "Belong here or not, a man should treat you like a woman in your line of work." He finished rolling a new cigarette and lit it with a match. He tossed the match into a pan on the table. He looked at her. "Women like you are probably here cause you need money. So why turn down a sure-thing?"

His frankness surprised her. "My line of work? Fuck you. I am not a whore. I don't want this."

"Well, seems strange then to find you in an establishment like this, then don't it. So, you need that money really bad, don't you?" His attention was clearly focused on her. His eye brows raised as he waited for her to answer.

"You're right, I do need money. I needed the money to leave this place," she said in a moment of brutal honesty.

Why she opened up about this to him she did not know. There was a knock on the door that broke the tension. Gunn put down the cigarette and walked to the door. It was a kitchen hand with the food he had ordered. There were two plates and forks. The roast smelled good. He took the food and placed it on the dresser. He closed the door and locked it and then brought the food over to the table. He set down the fork and knife on her plate and then his.

"Sit and eat," he said as he pulled out the chair across from the one he had sat in. The table was stained a dark color and looked to be made of oak. She was hungry and stood up from the bed and walked over to the table. He walked around her and sat across from her at the table. He divided the meat and potatoes amongst them with the cutting knife and the fork. As he picked up his fork, she began to say grace. He looked up at her and waited until she finished as he held his silverware and then began to eat. They sat in silence for several minutes.

"This is a good roast," she said to him as they had each half finished.

He nodded in agreement. He took another bite and swallowed. He looked up and said to her, "It is. Praying before grace, you're a believer then."

"I am, and you?"

"I left that a long time ago. Coming here was hard for you then, with that guilt and judgment and all."

"Conscience is a tricky thing."

"So, where you leaving to?"

"Colorado, my sister is leaving in two weeks' time. I need the money to travel with them." She spoke honestly and felt she could trust this man for some reason. He listened to her.

"Why is she leaving?" he asked. He finished a bite of his food and then pulled a long drag off a new rolled cigarette.

"She is moving their with her husband. I will have no family left here, and we have been living with our neighbor. Since our neighbor's wife died, the man took to drink."

He listened intently to the details and struggles she had endured through the dimly lit room. She looked at him and noticed how his beard extended about an inch lower than his jaw line. His eyes made him look weathered and old, but he didn't look old. His skin was tanned and leathered from the sun. He looked at her gently with curiosity. "Where is the plot?"

She continued, "About seventy miles from Denver."

"I hear it's nice there. I've only seen them mountains from a distance. What of the property here?"

"The bank is going to take back his property. Foreclosure notice came not too long ago. I had been saving for years behind his back in case I ever found a way out. He found the money I had been saving," she paused, and tears started to fall. It took her some moments to gather herself, "He gambled it away. So, here I am earning my ticket out."

He took the cloth napkin that his fork and knife had been wrapped in and handed it to her. He looked at her and saw a spirit near breaking.

"Like I said, I'm not much of a believer," he said in French. He did not like the man who stole from her. He was a weak man praying on innocence of this woman. "Why not marry him or someone around here?"

"He is lost and too old. Besides, at least like 'em if you do," she said. They both laughed.

"You have a good heart."

"I try. The thought of it makes me feel ugly on the inside," she said back to him.

It was at this moment he realized there was wine and glasses on the stand next to the bed. He stood up and went over and poured wine into the two wood cups on the stand. He handed one to her and sat back down.

He took his handkerchief and wiped her tears off her face.

"Well, you aren't ugly. Besides, you wouldn't want your first one to be that man anyway. He had rotten teeth." He looked at her eyes as he said it. She was beautiful he thought to himself.

The gesture calmed her nerves. She laughed at this and their meal. Both took a drink.

"He did," she said.

Everett sat back in his chair and put his feet up on the bed. She looked at him again. He listened as the rain hitting the roof seemed to get louder

There was a strong roar of thunder. "Storm is getting stronger."

"It is. Is your timing always this good?" she said with a smirk.

He took a watch out his pocket and tossed it to her. "What time is it?" he asked.

She caught it and looked at it "You can't tell time?"

"I can tell time. What time is it?" he repeated.

"It says half past six," she exclaimed as she looked at him confused. "This watch is broken."

"My timing is about as right as that watch," he said with a smile. She laughed.

"Why carry it then?" she asked him after she laughed. Her knee pulled up onto the chair, and she rested her head on her knee.

"It's the last thing I have from my father. It hasn't worked in years."

"That is sweet. What was he like?"

"He was a bastard. A mean son of bitch. From what I remember, I was about twelve when he left. My brother died the next year. Sister and mother died from typhoid a few years after that."

She moved off the chair and stood up. She felt comfortable now and was interested in this stranger.

"How old are you?" she asked.

"Old enough, I think I was born in '56 or '58," he replied back to her. He rolled another cigarette, licked it, and put it to his lips. She saw the scar on his right cheek that was faded and about two inches long. His hair was long and tucked behind his ears. None were gray, but certain parts looked darker than others. He took his feet off the bed as she sat on the bed next to him. He asked her no questions but just looked at her for a few seconds.

"Que?" she asked him in French. The thunder outside got louder. She took a drink and the silence continued. He turned and looked back out the window.

"How old are you?" he asked her. He took another match and went to strike it.

"Old enough," she said back to him playfully. "Please don't smoke another."

He stopped and paused. He looked at her and smirked. He put the match and cigarette into his pocket. "What are you hoping to do when you leave? After all this," he asked her while still looking out the window at the lighting and sky through the window. His back was to her now. She did not like this.

"Something."

"Something, that could be anything," he said back to her.

"Well, anything is better than nothing. All this here is nothing"

"Nothing can find a way to be everything."

"How is nothing, everything?" she asked him confused.

"When that happens, you will know," he said amused.

"Well, working on a farm won't be nothing. I'll dream up something, I suppose. The chance of that happening is as likely as a man flying."

"Or a man walking on the moon," he said and turned back to her. They both smiled.

"Yes, both of those would be nice things. But they are all dreams." She looked at him.

His eyes were weary, and he looked tired.

"Are you a dangerous man?" she asked him.

"When I have to be. We all do things we don't like," he said back to her. This wasn't a funny remark and just sat in the air. She was confused by this and felt afraid. He thought how beautiful she looked in the low-lit room. He was tired and took off his gun belts and shoulder holster. He placed them on the table.

"You don't have anything to worry about Ora. I am going to sleep."

She felt hurt by this, "Would you want to . . ."

He smiled at her, "I don't even know your name."

"My name is Ora Corbett. What is your name?"

"Everett Gunn. Enchanté, Ora."

"Enchanté,Everett."

"Now that you know my name. Would you like to . . ."

"I am honored, Ora, but I didn't bring you up here for that."

He walked around the bed and turned the oil lamp off and then went back to the chair where he sat to fall asleep.

"Oh," she replied embarrassed. "Good night, Everett."

"Goodnight Ora."

He closed his eyes, within moments he fell asleep. She felt upset by being turned down but had a strange respect for this man. She got under the covers and fell asleep flustered. She turned and looked at him as he lay asleep upright in the chair. Finally, she fell asleep.

The sound of rain still hitting the roof and breaking the silence.

He slept for a few hours and then woke as he always did. It was still dark out, but he increased the flame on the oil lamp. His back was stiff as it usually was in the mornings. Ora lay asleep on the bed. She was on her side and facing him. She looked at peace as her hair lay over her face. He stood up and put his holsters on. He tried to make as little noise as he could. The floorboards barely squeaked as he put out the oil lamp. He looked at her as she slept. The room was dark, but he could still see the outline of her face. He put his hand into his pocket that held his bill fold. He put $100 on the night stand next to the bed. She deserves more than this he thought.

He walked around the bed and unlocked the door with the key. He opened the door and stepped out into the hallway. He placed the key on the night stand. He felt the rush of regret in his stomach, but he had to be leaving to ride to the next meeting. Tell them you stay for three days and leave in two was his motto. It made every threat relax knowing they had two nights to make a run at you.

He closed the door and walked down to the front desk. There was a man there.

"I am turning in the key for the suite." Gunn said.

"You paid for three days though sir. We do not refund after payment," the clerk said.

"Keep the money. If the girl, Ora, wishes to stay, let her keep the room for the rest of what is paid for."

"Certainly, sir."

He motioned for him to come closer to whisper to him. "How was your evening? That one's a real whippersnapper?" he asked him very interested and with a wink.

Everett smiled and leaned in real close after looking both directions. He saw no one else in the lobby area. He motioned that he was going to whisper in the clerk's ear. As he did this, his hand went down to his gun belt and took his pistol out. He drew it up, cocked it, and pointed it so that the end of the gun was touching the man's temple. The clerk stared at him scared. There was silence for a few moments. The two men's eyes looked at each other. Suddenly, there was the sound of drizzling water on the floor. The clerk emptied his bladder onto himself.

"You talk about her like that again, I'll kill you.," Everett said to him.

The clerk nodded. Gunn released the hammer of the gun and holstered it. He let the clerk go and took a step towards the door and stopped.

"I will need something. I need a leave note for her. Get that pencil and paper."

The clerk turned and grabbed the pencil and paper. Everett took the pencil and paper and wrote something down on the note and folded it. He handed the note, the pad, and pencil back to the man.

"Make sure she gets that when she rises."

"Absolutely sir."

"Good. You pissed yourself, change your pants," Everett said back to him.

Chapter 6

The sunlight came through the window that faced east and north. It was still a cool morning before the heat would come. Ora woke and rubbed her eyes. She looked around the room. To her disappointment, she was alone. Besides the plates from the meal from the night before on the table, all traces of a second person were gone. He had left without so much as a goodbye. She pushed the blanket off herself and stood up onto the floor.

She had never met a man like him.

"Shit," she said out loud in French and shook her head. She wished she hadn't fallen asleep. He was a rough man, she thought. "Best he left when he did," she said aloud. Then she thought he was so gentle though. She turned and saw something on the nightstand. She gasped and grabbed her mouth.

There was a one-hundred-dollar bill. It was crinkled, but she had never seen anything so generous in her life. She slowly grabbed it off the nightstand and held it up to the light to look at it. She gasped and then smiled as her worries evaporated away and turned into excitement. Her hands shook. She folded it and put it her dress's pocket. She found her shoes on the floor and put them on. She opened the door and walked down the hall to the stairs. She reached the lobby but felt light-footed. She did not want to stop and see Madame Porcella or anyone else, so she tried to rush through the lobby. Halfway to the door, she heard the clerk shout.

"Wait, wait, Miss Ora. I've a correspondence for you!" someone shouted at her.

"That is quite all right. I have no need," she replied and turned back toward the door.

"Yes, yes, miss, you do!" he shouted back and ran from behind the counter toward her with the note outstretched in his hand. He almost fell over because he was off balance as he ran. She stopped, and he handed her the note. There was a yellow stain running down his light-tan-colored pants.

She looked at the urine stain on his pants. He noticed this and looked back at her blushing.

"He was quite insistent that you receive this."

"He was?" she asked, surprised and secretly delighted.

"He was."

"Is that what caused this?" she said, pointing to his pants, her finger making small circles as she pointed to the piss-stained area in discussion. She held back a small laugh as hard as she could.

He coughed and said nothing. He blushed and looked around, embarrassed to make eye contact.

"Yes, it is. As I said, he was very insistent."

"Mister, you need to change your pants," she said, now releasing her laugh. "Thank you."

She turned and walked out through the front door, laughing. What a character Everett is, she thought. He was bold, crude, but still gentle.

The clerk said nothing and went into the back room and did his best to find a clean pair of pants. There were none on shelves in the back room for him to wear. He cursed out loud and considered if he could get away without wearing any pants for the day. Then he came to his senses and splashed vodka on the pants to cut the smell of his own urine. Better to be known as drunk than pissing in one's own pants, he said to himself.

She walked down toward the stable to get her horse. She paused outside the barbershop and sat on a small bench. The bench leaned toward one side and felt rickety. She opened the note. It was written in poor handwriting:

Ora,

I hope you found the money on the nightstand.
Take it and use it for whatever you like. I hope it
is enough to give you the freedom to travel with
your sister. Put it in the bank deposit box. I enjoyed
your company. I will return in 14 days. I will be at
the saloon. I hope to see you again.

Everett

She smiled as she read this and felt slightly torn. Looking up,
she realized Everett was right. Bringing the money home was not
prudent. She thought of the bank. She had never been able to have
an account before, but this was enough money to open an account
she thought. She stood up and walked across the street toward the
savings and loan bank. She opened the door and walked inside.
It had dark wood edging and paintings on the wall. There were
metal bars all over the place for protection for the safe and staff.
The workers were giving her strange looks as she did not look like
she belonged.

A man walked up to her.

"May I help you, miss?"

"I would like to deposit some money in a safe deposit box."

"Well, you are in the right place then. My name is Woodford
Thesman. Follow me this way." He led her to the counter. He had
on a dark wool suit and red tie. He held his suspenders as he
walked. "Jimmy, can you help this lady?"

"Absolutely, Mr. Thesman. Hello, miss, what can I help you
with today?"

"I would like to buy a safe deposit box," she repeated to Mr.
Thesman.

"Oh, you don't buy a safe deposit box, you rent it. For how
long would like to rent it?" he corrected her snootily. He wore a
dark suit and small glasses that rested on the bridge of his nose.
He tapped a pen nervously as she sat across from him.

She was embarrassed, not knowing what to do. "Oh, for one
month, please."

"All right, short-term rental. That will be ten cents, but first, I need your name and whether or not you would like us to keep the key."

"Ora Corbett, I would like you to keep the key," she said back to him and spelled out her name to him.

He took out the forms and had her sign her name in a few places. She took out the hundred-dollar bill and asked for him to break it into change. His eyes got wide when he saw the money. Judgment came over his eyes as he looked back up to her.

She felt judged but did not care. You would pay to sleep with me, she thought and almost said it out loud. It didn't matter though. She had not compromised herself, and by some stroke of divine intervention, this man had saved her before she had to do that. She signed the documents with the pen. She paid the rental fee, kept two 5-dollar bills and the rest brought with her to the safe deposit box. It was number 1123. She took the key and opened the lock. The door swung open, and she took the box out. She turned and put it on the table. She put the money and his note inside. It would be safe here, she thought, and I will get to leave with my sister. She put the box back into the safe and locked it. She felt empowered in that moment, and her face had a proud smile.

She went back out to the lobby. She handed the key back to the clerk. His eyes looked at her again with judgment. She handed the key back to him.

"Thank you for your business, miss," the clerk said.

"Thank you for your help." She cursed him in her head in French. Pute ah, she thought.

She turned and walked outside. She went down to the bathhouse and paid for a bath with warm water. This cost ten cents. She felt clean and refreshed after this. She dressed and then went down to the stable to get Maple. She and the stable hand exchanged pleasantries as he put the saddle on the horse. She tipped him five cents and mounted the horse.

She kicked the horse and was off the road to their home. The sun was shining, and the wind cut through her hair. It was still damp but was drying in the wind. She looked wild. She turned Maple loose as they rounded the creek and met the open field. She prayed to herself, saying thank you. The colors of the flowers that stood tall behind patches of the purple lavender plants, the sky, and even the leaves seemed brighter than even a day before.

She got to the fork on the path and decided to turn toward Samuel's place to visit her sister. She pushed Maple hard the last mile and a half from there to get to the cottage. When the ranch was in view, she slowed and let the horse trot the last hundred yards or so. She tied the horse to the fence post near the house.

Her sister was outside and waved to her. "Ora!" she said.

Ora said nothing and hugged her. "Loren, how are you?"

"I am well today," Loren replied. "You seem excited. Is everything all right?"

"I have fantastic news. I have the money and some extra. I will be able to make the journey with you." She felt happy but apprehensive. Her sister continued on with the conversation, but Ora couldn't comprehend any of it. She thought about the man she had met the night before, the drifter who without so much as asking anything in return.

"Ora, are you listening to me, honey!" Loren said to her.

"Oh, I am sorry. What were you saying?"

Loren laughed. "Samuel heard you were at the establishment last night."

"I was," she replied. She blushed with embarrassment. "Not in the way you would expect."

"Ora!" Loren said with concern on her face. "Are you all right? I never would have expected that. We could have found a way to—"

"Stop, it is okay, and there was no way I could have gone without the money," she replied.

"You're right," Loren said, "but you went there of all places and you made up the difference in one night?"

"I did," she replied, embarrassed. "A stranger took care of me."

"Took care of you? What do you mean?"

Ora started to speak but couldn't find the words.

Loren cut her off and said, "Tell me the details! What did he look like? How was his performance?" she said while making a gesture with her hands.

Ora blushed and laughed with her sister. "It was none of that. There was this awful cowboy. He held me tight and kept trying to get me to take him upstairs. I couldn't go through with it, so I stalled him and resisted." Loren listened to every word with more anticipation and concern. Ora continued, "He became frustrated and began to grab and insult me. I swore at him in French."

"In French," Loren said. "Porque Francais?"

"Yes, in French," Ora said.

"Not in English?" Loren said.

"That is what I said," Ora said. Her eyes grew stern.

"You said French," Loren replied. "Don't get upset with me."

"You frustrate me when you don't listen. Now, I thought of Mama, and it just came out of me and then the Madame came over and was offering me up as a free one for the trouble. Anything he wanted," Ora said.

"Anything he wanted! Men are so sick, that would have been terrible. That sort of thing with a man you love can get uncomfortable," Loren said.

"I know! Before this happened with the Madame, this stranger was standing at the bar and heard him called me a whore."

"He called you a whore?"

"He did, and then the stranger hit the cowboy over the head with his pistol. The cowboy fell to the floor, and the stranger got him to apologize to me."

"How did he do that?" she asked.

"He pointed the pistol at his head," Ora said.

"A total stranger knocked another man to the ground over insulting you? That is quite an exciting night," Loren said.

"He was something. He paid the Madame and then spoke French to me and brought me upstairs," Ora said.

"He spoke French. What happened upstairs?" Loren said with a laugh.

"Nothing, we just talked," Ora said. She pulled her hair behind her ear.

"Really, you two just talked? I would have hopped on him right quick after a display like that," Loren said.

"I know you would have," Ora said with a laugh. Loren had hopped on many men in her time before meeting Samuel.

"Well, what happened then?" Loren asked.

"Well, he asked about why I was working there. He had food brought up to the room, and we had dinner. We talked in French the entire time. I told him about my life. I fell asleep on the bed after he fell asleep in the chair. When I woke up the next morning, he was gone but had left a hundred dollars on the nightstand."

"You had dinner and talked and then went to sleep and had a hundred dollars waiting for you the next morning? You are a liar! You were turning parlor tricks on him all night, weren't you?" her sister exclaimed.

"Honest to God's truth," she said back.

"You are telling the truth! Was he handsome at least?" she asked as she read her sister's eyes.

"He looked rugged, in a different way. He moved gingerly. He had long light-brown hair with some gray in it. He had narrow eyes. He had a beard that was not kept. He looked weathered but thin," Ora replied.

"He was your knight in shining armor," Loren said to her.

"If knights came wearing jackets, cowboy hats, and smelled like he had not bathed in several days, then yes, he was my knight in shining armor," Ora quipped. Both laughed at this.

"Will you see him again?" Loren asked. She asked this, and Ora stopped. Her heart paused, and she didn't know how to answer. She looked past Loren. "Well, will you, sister?"

"I won't see him again, Loren. He won't be back until after we leave for Colorado. I am not waiting on him," Ora said. She hid her devastation from her sister like the camouflage of a lion on the Serengeti . Loren studied her.

"Well, it wasn't meant to be, but he is an angel nonetheless," Loren said. "I wish I could have met him."

"You would have been impressed, but you have Samuel," Ora said.

"I do have my Samuel. I love him, but he does get absentminded from time to time. He should be back soon for dinner tonight. Would you like to stay for dinner?"

"I would love to," she said back to her.

"That is great. I will just set out another plate. This man did nothing with you. He must have a war injury or enjoys long nights," Loren said with a laugh. They went inside and began preparing supper. They hadn't been able to enjoy each other's company like that for some time.

Chapter 7

The sun began to fall into the sky, and soon it would begin tucking itself into the horizon. He could see from his window the capital building in Philadelphia. The orange color cast the rays out while the warmth from the sun slowly began to fade. He could feel the temperature change in his office. The candlelight flickered on both edges of his desk. The light from the ceiling lamp fell upon the room. He twisted the pen in his hand before he went to dip it into the ink. After tapping it twice on the desk, he set it down and turned toward the mantel behind his chair. He took the decanter and placed it on his desk. He turned back and grabbed one of the three glasses. He poured three fingers of whiskey into glass and took a drink. He felt it warm his bones and stung his stomach like the poison of a snake. He took another drink and then set the glass back down. His focus returned to the bill on this desk. He adjusted his reading glasses.

He thought to himself that both parties in the house had worked together on a bill that would make water travel and commerce easier in the state. He thought to himself that this bill would make Pennsylvania more competitive for interstate commerce. He looked out the window to see the sunset again. The colors in the sky matched the feeling he felt from the glass of whiskey. He knew there would be some retaliation from North Eastern States, but it would take at least a year to a year and a half to see a bill signed into law. The risk was worth it for the people. He poured another glass and took it down in one gulp.

He stood up from his desk and moved the decanter back on the mantel. He walked out of his office into the common area. "It is a good day to be governor," he said as he smiled toward his secretary, Margaret.

"You took a long time to sign that bill. The papers are waiting outside to get a statement from you. Do you have anything prepared?"

He handed her the bill as she was speaking and ignored her comment. "Please see to it that Herman brings this back to the chambers tomorrow."

"Absolutely," she said. "But the papers, Governor?"

"Papers, more like vultures. Yes, yes, we will have to speak with the press. God, how I love the First Amendment. Craw in my backside," he said as he put on his coat. "Have a good evening, Margaret."

"You too, Governor," she replied.

He put on his top hat and left his office. He walked down the long hall to the front entrance of the building. There was dust on the wood floor plants from the dried mud of the day before. The lamps on the side walls had been lit. He was nearing the front entrance now. There would be several journalists for the papers waiting eagerly for any bit of news. They were the same familiar faces that praise you one minute and then stab you in the back the next. He said good night to several aides still in the state building inside the doors until he finally reached for the door. He saw the journalist gathered around, and each eagerly had their hand up for questions.

"I will not be answering any questions about the legislation today. It was signed into law not twenty minutes ago. Our Senate and House worked together over the last several months to bring forth legislation that will increase commerce in our fine state by lowering interstate tariffs for transport on waterways and rails. We will be seeing more jobs come to our fine state, and the people deserve it," he said. He denied answering questions and then walked through the crowd, even bumping shoulders with some men in the crowd until he walked toward the carriage.

His protection, two soldiers always traveled will him, one inside the carriage and one with the driver. Both had the last name Caldwell. Both were tall, lean, and had the first name John, except one spelled his name without the letter "h". Both were of similar temperament, but neither was related to the other. The governor at first found it frustrating having them with the same name but soon found it amusing as he would call for one's attention and both heads would turn. He finally learned the blond Caldwell's middle name was Milton. He called him Milt for short.

"Mr. McCree! Good evening."

"Evening, Governor! Where shall we ride to this evening?" McCree asked in response.

"Take us to the Landing, I have a business meeting there at half past six."

"Absolutely, sir. Right away," McCree replied. He closed the door after Milt joined the governor in the carriage. John joined McCree in the shotgun seat. The carriage started away. John and McCree had developed a report together. Each enjoyed the company of the other and enjoyed smoking rolled cigarettes. The horses plodded through the mud at a respectable pace. The streets got busier as they headed toward this particular tavern.

The governor did not say a word to Milt for most of the ride. Nearing the end, he asked him about his family and their newborn baby. Milt appreciated the interest and informed him that she was in good health and his wife had recovered quickly from her illness.

"She is a tough Irish lass," the governor said, joking.

"That she is, sir, temper to match," Milt replied as they both laughed. The governor jokingly nudged Milt's shoulder with his elbow as they laughed. The carriage was slowing.

"We're here, sir," McCree said as the carriage halted. The Landing was made of stone, so they did not have to step into the street. It was a relief to not have one's ankles covered in mud, the governor thought.

"McCree, would you return at half past nine. I don't expect this to take so long," the governor said.

"Not a problem, sir. I will be at the tavern down the road," McCree replied.

"Take this and get yourself a warm meal," the governor said as he placed a dollar bill in his hand.

"Thank you, sir," McCree said. He appreciated his generosity.

"Caldwells," the governor said as he turned back to them while motioning inside, "let's find ourselves a table near the fire."

Both agreed with him, and one moved in front and opened the door, and the other went behind. They had done this so many times it was a well-oiled machine. Their usual booth was not occupied. The owner in fact had saved it for this very occasion. Being left-handed, Milt would stand to the opposite side of the governor facing the door, and John would stand on the right. A glass of Scotch was brought to the table as he sat down. It was a fifteen-year from the Highlands of Scotland, the very best they had available. In reality, it had a bite but finished smooth with the right amount of peatiness. A lager was brought for each of the Caldwells to enjoy as well in tall clean glasses.

The Landing had wallpaper on the walls a French classical pattern. The overhead lanterns were scattered across the ceiling in a pattern that would allow tables to be placed under them. The booths along the side walls each had a candlelight on the wall. The tables were well-finished oak round tables. The floor had tiles laid in pattern with black-and-white circular patterns. The light radiated enough to allow everyone to have their privacy. A band would begin playing after seven in the evening. This is why the Landing was a preferred place to discuss business matters in public. You could understand your associate but not be heard by anyone in the gallery.

The governor sipped his drink and sat alone saying nothing at the table. He made no indication he wanted to acknowledge anything. He took out a pad of paper he had that he kept in his right front pocket and began reading it intently. These were his notes for the meeting that was not minutes away, here in this poorly lit and damp-smelling bar. He learned that as a younger man clerking for the district judge after law school, politics is most lethal and effective when it's conducted in the dark. It was this game of cat and mouse from these dealings and understandings that he loved more than the power he yielded. You could measure a man and his resolve by reading his face as each side would trade information. He had become a master through his years at not showing anything and at reading the meaning of each shift of his opposition's body. It was this skill and willingness to get dirty that had saved the state more money than he could count by the leverage he had gained at this very table—this uneven oak table that sat in this damp and dark room. That is why it was known as "the rack" to those in the political world in Pennsylvania. You were going to get stretched, and it was going to hurt. A man had even taken a swing at him in the past. Unfortunately for that man, the governor had grown up boxing at school and knocked him out with a quick left hook.

Mr. Allencort entered the Landing at precisely half past six. He had never been to this establishment but could see the guards across the tavern to his right. He had worn his black wool jacket over his blue suit with a slightly darker blue tie. He had looked forward to this meeting all day and was not nervous at all because he felt prepared. The hostess greeted him, and he thanked her. He told her, "I am here to meet the governor."

"Right this way, sir." The woman led him over to the governor's table. The Caldwells looked at him as they each sipped their ale.

"Governor, Mr. Allencort is here for you," she said.

"Thank you, Theresa," the governor replied as he looked at her and then to Allencort. His left hand was holding his glass of whiskey and then set it down. He stood up and extended his hand. "Mr. Allencort, pleased to finally meet you in person after so much correspondence."

"Pleasure to meet you as well. Call me Percy, Governor."

"Are you a Scotch drinker, Percy?" the governor asked.

"I keep a bottle at the office and at home," he replied.

"Fantastic! Theresa, can we have one more glass brought for us?"

"Certainly, I will be right back," she replied.

Percy sat down across from him. He surveyed the booth, the room, and the Caldwells. He thought to himself, This is the great rack where the governor had negotiated so many deals and won nearly all of them? I am not impressed. Both men then looked at each other and sat in silence. The governor knew what he was thinking and held back his smile as he thought, I am going to crush this son of a bitch.

The governor always spoke second and felt very comfortable sitting in silence. Theresa brought a new glass and set in the table in front of Percy. She poured him a glass. Both men nodded and looked up at her. The noise of the room overtook them, and seconds turned into minutes. The governor did not touch his glass. Percy finally succumbed to the discomfort of the silence, and he sipped his drink.

"This is a very smooth," he quipped. "Is it from the lowlands?"

"It is smooth, and I am not sure. It is good though," he replied. This bastard doesn't know his scotch. He took a drink. "Damn good stuff though. "

Percy took another drink and set his glass back down. He spoke with his hands as men often do to deal with being nervous. "We wish to expand our operations through Pennsylvania into Ohio. With the growing market west, we need to keep expanding. Cincinnati and Cleveland would be prime locations for our company to begin bringing coal into, especially with this new legislation that may be passed any day now." He sipped and calmly waited for a reply.

"Percy, it is rude to begin talking business before the second glass of Scotch. Waiter, may we try your selection from the Islay, please. I believe it was the ten-year. Thank you." He turned his attention back to Percy.

"Forgive me," he said and finished his first glass.

"We have several companies that are vying for positions for coal transportation through Pennsylvania into Ohio with this new legislation. I have heard of your company, but what makes your company the best option? From what I gather, your operations refuse to work with local vendors, and that keeps money out of citizens' pockets. Keeps our wages down."

"That we do, and I defend this practice as common to remain competitive and what is best for the company. There is risk in river and rail travel. In order to exist in a business with competition such as ours, you have to keep our labor costs down. Whether it is our company or another, there will be labor brought in from out of state."

The governor had leaned back in his chair, and Percy saw his demeanor change from his face. The light shifted ever so lightly. His looked turned cold. The waiter brought the new Scotch over and took off the cork. She poured the Scotch into each glass and then corked the bottle. The room, with all its noise, in that booth was completely silent. Neither man looked away from the other as their glasses were filled, and the waiter walked away.

"You speak as if you are certain of your situation, your fortune laid upon your feet," the governor quipped.

"Our board feels confident in our proposal," he said to the governor with a smile.

"Then why are they not here?" the governor asked.

Percy started to sweat now. "They were unable to arrange to make this trip."

"They could not make reservations." He laughed out loud. Then his face went back to seriousness. "Your company stands to grow exponentially by moving into Ohio through Pennsylvania, and from your proposition moments ago, your practice is standard and therefore should be of a strength to you." He paused. "Yet you sit alone, no leverage, no power." The governor paused and took a drink before he began again.

His eyes darkened. "You said yourself there are several companies vying to be the first into our city. Your practice discriminates against the people of Pennsylvania. You think I am just going to allow a company to walk right into our state and allow outsiders to leave with Pennsylvania's money because it is standard practice?" he asked this rhetorically. Percy stumbled as he tried to determine what to say in response. Nothing came to him, so he put his hands on the table. The governor's voice had remained calm the entire time as he stood to leave. Percy took two steps away from the table and then turned around after he exited the booth. Percy thought about how he wanted to stab this man through his neck at that moment.

"Governor, I apologize. We can be flexible with our methods," he pleaded to the governor after he turned back around. He feared for his job.

"Go on, I didn't want to waste enjoying my drink," he said in reply without turning around. Percy sat back down across from him.

"What recommendations can I bring back to my board?" he asked.

The governor took a sip before speaking. "I need two-thirds of your labor to come from the people of Pennsylvania. I also need your company to partner with the Timber Red Trust Company for your off-loading at the ports and rail stations. They own a different company, the Five Star Partners, which is regional in several states. If at any point this arrangement is not followed, your license will be suspended permanently."

Percy replied, "I have heard of the Five Point Partners. They are a conglomerate in several trades. This arrangement will be difficult to approve because we have some competition with them in New York."

"The out-of-state transport tax was dropped by 15 percent today. If you want this opportunity, you will do what the fuck I say when I say it in this state," the governor retorted.

Percy's face could not hide the disappointment. "We were expecting a more meaningful decrease. We listen well."

"Meaningful, I think the Jackson and Curtis Company will be happy to handle this transport for us through the state and be open to our state contracts," the governor stated calmly.

"The Jackson and Curtis Company, their license was revoked!" he said in shock.

"It happened to be reinstated today," the governor said and laid it on the table. It shook Percy as this was their largest competitor in New England.

"All right, the 15 percent will do just nicely," Percy said.

"That is what I thought," the governor said. "In addition, contracts with the Five Points are given preferential treatment in government contracts because of their involvement with the Civil War and hiring of veterans afterwards. That bill runs out in five years. Lastly, I will need your company to donate to the local hospital and university an amount of one thousand dollars in the spring each year." The governor at last finished another sip of his drink. He stood and said as he looked down at Percy, "I am going to have a gentleman travel to your headquarters from Timber Red Trust. He has a document with the terms I have just discussed. Take it to your board and have it signed and returned in seven days, and this opportunity is yours."

Percy maintained his focus on the governor and realized how small he was compared to this man in this moment. "I will have it returned to you with signature before the end of the week."

"Good, now enjoy yourself in our fine town, Mr. Allencort." The governor shook his hand firmly, and the men locked eyes.

The governor said without saying, You are nothing and I have crushed you. He owned a small percentage of both companies through a shell company. Politically, this would provide jobs to the local voting population that were more expensive than their labor coming from West Virginia. Not allowing them to handle material at the ports and rail yards would bring in more tax dollars as well.

The governor turned and walked toward the door. He handed a two-dollar bill to cover the drinks to the owner. The Caldwells were in front of him, and one opened the door. The carriage was waiting for him, and he entered.

"Well done, sir."

"I would have settled for 50 percent local work had he not been such a New York prick."

"Fine job, sir," Caldwell shot back. "New York prick. Ha, very clever, sir."

"Fine, indeed," the governor said with a laugh. He made another joke, and the men went on their way.

Back inside the bar, Percy was staring at the contract that had been handed to him after the governor had left. It clearly stated that operations would be run out of the building owned by Timber Red and that outside of management, two-thirds of employees would be from Pennsylvania and the remaining would be outsourced to Five Points. This effectively made them deliver the coal to these companies at low margins, and they could not set foot on the dock or in the shipyards. He realized that these were the only terms he could bring back to his board, and it would likely cost him his job.

Chapter 8

She woke before the roosters announced the morning. The fescue grass was still covered in dew and felt cold and wet, and the sky was still dark. Some clouds had covered the moon during the night, but now the sky was clear. She stayed in bed and lay on her right side, simply staring at the wall. Her hands curled tightly around the edge of the dark wool blanket. Her face wore no expression. She lay there like this for almost an hour.

Finally, she pulled the blanket back and sat up from her bed. Her feet were still covered by the blanket. The air was cool, and the hair on her arms rose as her skin tightened to form bumps. She slid her feet onto the floor and then stood up. The floor was cold as well. She put on a sweater over her nightgown that was hanging on the dresser and found a pair of socks to put on her feet. There was a pair of overalls, and she slid those over her legs. She felt warm. The house was still dark, but some light came through the window, lighting the kitchen floor down the hallway. She was careful with each step to not disturb the floorboards. She made it to the kitchen and then finally to the door.

She pulled the sleeves of the wool sweater over her hands to keep them warm from the cold air. She breathed into her hands to warm them and stepped off the porch onto the ground. She walked through the fescue grass out away from the house until she reached an old elm tree. It was her tree. She rested her back against the tree and pulled her legs into her chest. The grass underneath her was crushed and worn away from the time she had spent sitting there. The bugs and crickets made their noises from the weeds and grass down the hill in front of her. The trees all around the clearing kept her isolated and trapped, except for this glance out from the top of the hill. It had always been a sort of prison, the hills holding everything in because of the trees.

In the distance, she saw a red-tailed hawk gliding through the air. She closed her eyes and drifted off to sleep against the tree. The sun continued to rise. She fell back asleep against the tree until the sun rose high enough to reach her eyes through the shade of the tree. It pierced her eyes, and she squinted to protect them from the sun's rays. She scratched her forehead and extended her legs and yawned. She thought about leaving with her sister and the homestead on a stream at the base of the Rocky Mountains surrounded by trees. There she thought, the sun would slowly rise each morning over the hills through the trees and then fall down into the horizon. It would all be different, but it would be the same for her in Colorado she had thought these last two weeks. Her heart and dreams would remain unchanged, still searching for some purpose or desire. She sat and continued to think about questions she had not tried to answer in a long time. In her heart, she knew she didn't want to be the same.

She continued to lean against the tree. The money from Everett still sat in the safe deposit box. She had never gone to collect it. She had folded her clothes in stacks on her dresser, and her other belongings sat in a chest in her room the night before. She had tried for so long to leave, and now that she had the means and opportunity, it didn't excite her. Instead, she thought about Everett and how speaking French with him reminded her of her mother. It felt like an anchor had been thrown into the water, holding her in place.

The sun had fully risen now and brought the warmth back to her face. She stood up and went back inside the house. The grass felt drier now on her hands and bare feet. She walked into the house and coursed over to the kitchen to make coffee. While the water heated up over the stove, she ate some pieces of bread with jam. The coffee was finished, and she poured a cup for herself. She savored the taste and put in some stale sugar.

She had some time before her sister would arrive to pick her up. She went to the water urn and poured some water into the basin. She splashed some on her face and then washed it. She went back into the kitchen and began to boil water in a pot to make some vegetable stew. All they had left were carrots, potatoes, onions, and radishes from their garden. She washed the dirt off them with care. It took some time to dice them. Then as the water boiled, she dropped in flour and the vegetables with a little butter. Then she added salt and pepper. It was not much but would have to do, she thought.

The neighbor had not been home for three days. He had sold the last of the oxen for money the week before. The chickens were underfed and had stopped laying eggs. She would love to have eggs to eat or, for that matter, something other the vegetable soup or just another variation of potatoes. One day soon, she thought she would treat herself.

The soup continued to cook, and she sliced the rye bread. It was firm and had sat in the bread cupboard for two days. The neighbor returned from his absence as she sliced the bread. His shirt was unbuttoned, and his eyes appeared heavy. Ora could smell his breath from across the room. Whiskey has the kind of odor that only seems pleasant in dark poorly lit rooms. This was not that place or that time.

"Your sister leaving today?" he asked as he sat down after he poured himself a glass of water.

She answered him in French in her head but spoke in English. "Yes, I believe so. She said she would by today to say goodbye."

He took a sip of his water and put his feet up on the table. "You goin' with her?" he asked in a patronizing tone. He showed no emotion on his face as he stared toward the wall before making eye contact with her.

"No, I won't be," she replied. She did her best to hold back the resentment she felt inside of her.

"Why not?" he asked her. She didn't answer him, but she looked over at him and bottled up her contempt as best she could. Her face turned red. He repeated the question again.

She didn't want to irritate him, so she answered him, "Je ne peux pas me le permettre." She did answer him like this to insult him. He looked at her.

"In English, dammit! Whatever the shit that is!" he shouted back at her.

"I . . . don't have the money to go," she answered him, knowing this was a lie. She wanted to throw her opportunity in his face but held back as best she could. She tapped her heel on the floor to maintain her composure. She turned to him.

He was laughing at her now. He was shaking his head, and when he smiled, he showed his teeth. "I know you don't. Sure went to good use though, and he took a small flask out from under his jacket."

She didn't respond and went back to stirring the soup, but her fingers were white from clenching the spoon. "It will be fine to stay here." This caught him off guard, and he took his feet off the table and seemed sick. He walked out onto the porch and vomited next to the house. Serves him right, she thought to herself. The soup would be ready soon enough, and Ora added a few more spices. She went to her room and changed into one of her dresses she had. She laid the overalls and sweater on the wood bench at the foot of the bed. She looked at herself in the mirror. She pulled her hair back into a ponytail.

Today may be the last day I will see my sister, she thought. It ought to be a good memory. "So look proper," she said to herself aloud. Her skin was slightly tanned from all the riding she had done lately. She felt exhausted and out of sorts, but Everett crept into her mind again. He might not return to town, but it still felt like an anchor had been planted in her heart that night and it wasn't going to let her move. She could always leave later and see if she could catch them, she lied to herself.

Sometime later, the sound of a wagon came from the road. The noise of the wheels rolling over uneven ground caused it to creak. The wood almost sounded like popcorn. Her sister's commands to the horses and the horse's noises grew louder and louder. Ora went to her room and gathered one of the trinkets her mother had given her before she died. Loren and Samuel approached. The wagon was loaded tall and tight. The seat springs bounced as the path was not level from divots and rocks. There were four horses leading the wagon and two cows tied to the wagon that followed in the rear. Ora waved from the porch to her sister. Both wore dresses of the same color.

"Oh, how wonderful, we're matching," Loren said with a glowing smile.

"We always think alike," Ora said back to her. "But you always follow my lead."

Loren got off the wagon and came and hugged Ora. "No, I don't, sister. It is you who follow me." Loren paused and looked around behind Ora. "Where are your things?" she asked as she saw no bags on the porch.

Ora looked at her. In the background were the wagon and her sister's husband. She saw the blue sky through the trees and was thankful this goodbye was in the shade that the trees provided. She didn't want the memory to be ruined by squinting eyes looking into the sunlight. "They are inside," Ora said.

"Well, go get them, Ora! We need to be getting on." There was a grain of confusion and a kernel of fear in her voice. Loren took a second to realize what was happening.

"I didn't pack them. You need to get on going," Ora said. She smiled at Loren with a sad smile, the kind of smile that spoke but did so without any words.

Loren nodded as she understood what she was really saying. Tears started in each of the eyes. She brought her hands to her eyes to wipe the tears. They hugged each other there in the shade. They didn't need to speak as they each knew how each other felt. "I will miss you, sister, and think of you often," Loren said.

"I will miss you too," Ora said back to her. "Now get out of here. Go live your life, and when you think of this place, think of the good times."

"I promise," Loren said as they held each other and then looked at each other. "Will I see you again?"

"Someday," Ora said to her. "I love you, sis."

"I love you too," Loren said. Both had a tear fall down their eyes.

They broke their embrace. Loren walked back to the wagon. She spoke to her husband. He nodded as she spoke. He looked at Ora with a sad smile and nodded to her. He took the reins and turned the wagon around. This took some time, and Ora just stood on the porch and watched them. As the wagon rode off away from the house, her sister turned to look back at Ora. They waved to each other. Ora didn't move from the porch for some time; she just stared down the road.

Chapter 9

Through the hills and toward the plain he road. He found himself tired and exhausted as he had several weeks before. His horse looked thinner as there had not been much to eat, and they had traveled hard and fast. Vernon and he had collected land deeds on failed businesses and farms in Kentucky and Indiana. All had gone much smoother than the first job. There had only been one shootout, and no one had died.

The last several weeks, Gunn had grown to enjoy his partner's company. They had spent some time drinking in saloons, and he had seen Vernon had a way with people. Both played cards and kept as low a profile as possible. It was obvious when they had met on the train (but also after they had worked together some more) that Vernon was an educated man. Educated men rarely sought out the fringe of society, but Gunn did not question Vernon's motivation as he could only relate to the feeling that he saw in himself as well. None of it mattered. The violence, the anger, and the predatory nature of it all didn't matter and had no consequence. One day, for better or worse, it would all be over, and someone else would take your place doing the same thing, filling the same purpose he had carried. It was this that let Gunn fall asleep at night without a troubled mind. Gunn knew he would have no issues with Vernon so long as they were in step with that reality.

Before they had departed, Vernon had told him he would not be needed for some time until a run of collections west in several months' time. Their last job had delayed him, and he had decided to return to the town outside Cincinnati in Ohio. He knew she would be gone, but he felt that he had to try to see her again. Despite being tired, he continued to push the horse.

"You've earned some good grain and rest," Gunn said aloud to the horse. He held the reins in his left hand and scratched the horse's neck with his right hand as he leaned forward, allowing the horse to take a short rest. The leather gloves kept his hands warm from the chill. He was glad to have them. Soon they continued on. Gunn's hair flopped from under his hat as he rode into town. It was late in the morning and still cool out. The last of the dew clung to the grass on the ground. The previous night had been cold. When his hands had touched the gunmetal, they nearly froze to it. He wished he had been able to start a fire.

Soon enough, he reached the town, and his horse trotted down the main street. The dirt and dust kicked up with each step until he reached the stable. Gunn dismounted and was greeted by the stable boy. He paid him to feed and brush the horse.

"Make sure he gets the best grain you have," Gunn said and then handed a tip to the boy.

"Yes, mister. We only have one kind though," the boy said.

Gunn, amused by his honesty, replied, "Well, just find him something extra, an apple then or a carrot." The regular townsfolk remembered him from his last visit into town and stared at him. It was as if he was one of the early frontier celebrities, like Davy Crockett. They all kept their distance from him. I sure am keeping that low profile, he thought to himself. It was half past ten, and he felt hungry. He saw the sign down the street for the café and walked toward it. He could smell coffee and food coming from the kitchen through the front door before he entered. He pushed the door open and went inside.

"Mister," the woman said behind the counter with a nod as she wiped plates clean with a rag.

"Morning!" Gunn said. "How fresh is the coffee?" he asked her.

"Brewed this morning, some of the best around. Do you want a booth or a seat at the table?" she asked him.

"Booth, miss," he said back to her. He took off his hat and ran his hands through his hair as he followed her. She led him to a small booth along the wall. He thanked her as he slid into the booth. The seat was covered in a rough cloth over the wood. It was not comfortable to sit in, but that didn't matter. It still felt good. His back ached, and he leaned on the wall to ease the pain. He looked around, and the walls were made of rough wide wooden planks. Sunlight shone in some gaps. A wood burning stove was in the corner and kicked heat into the tavern. The counter was sanded and smooth. It looked like it came from a walnut tree. There were plates and fine china behind the counter. It was a regular café that every small town had all over.

A few minutes passed, and then the woman walked up to his booth. She placed a cup in front of him and then poured him some coffee. The steam rose from the coffee as well as the aroma. She looked plain and had some gray hair speckled in her dark hair. He looked at her, and she smiled. "Would you like some breakfast?" she asked.

"I would. What's available today?" he replied.

She squinted her right eye and looked up to the left as she listed off the items. They included bacon, sausage, biscuit, bread pudding, and gravy.

"All that sounds goods. Thank you," he replied. He kept his gaze on the woman as she nodded. She walked away.

He sipped his coffee. It was hot and tasted good. He took his gloves off and flexed his hands. His face relaxed, and he took deep breaths as he rubbed his eyes. The tops of his hands were dirty. He took another sip and rubbed the middle of his palm with the other hand's thumb for a few moments. His rifle was placed on the edge of the booth closest to the wall. He put his hand behind his neck and then rubbed the knots of his neck out with his fingers. The ache stayed the same.

He sat alone and slowly sipped the coffee while he waited for his food. The woman brought him his breakfast and some silverware. She took a spare cloth napkin from her bag and gave it to him as well. She brought the kettle back and poured him some more coffee. He thanked her with a nod because his mouth was full of food. The food was sizzling and smelled good. There was a hint of lard and grease. He took the fork and knife and cut up a piece of sausage and ate it. He took a moment to savor it. It's good, he thought. As he continued to eat, some of the coffee was in his beard above his lip. He wiped it off on the napkin. He stared at the space across from him in the booth and thought the seat looked empty for some reason. He paused and then went back to his food. He knew he was late and that she had probably left with her sister. It had been stupid of him to return. This thought was a disappointment. He finished his meal and paid the woman.

He walked out into the street and went over to the wash parlor that was behind the saloon. He paid for a bath and washed himself in the privy. There was a bloodstain on his pant leg. He washed this as well and got some of it out. It was warmer out, and it helped dry him quickly after his bath. With all the excitement of the different jobs and collections he had been on, he felt bored. He dressed and then walked over into the saloon.

As he opened the door, he went to the right and over to the lobby area. The clerk was there, the one he had scared two weeks prior. The clerk stood up as he saw Gunn and adjusted his glasses. He fidgeted and shook in his shoes as Gunn approached.

"Do you have a room available?" Gunn asked.

"Yes, sir, certainly, sir," he said back. He read through the logbook. "Just a regular room this time."

"That will do just fine," Gunn said. Gunn looked down at the man's pants. He had on the same pair, but the stain from his urine had been washed out.

"All right, sign here, and here is the key," the clerk said as he handed him the key.

"I see you washed your pants, friend," Gunn said to him with a smile.

"I did, sir, and got your message to Miss Corbett," the clerk said.

"You did, good. Corbett? That is her maiden name?" Gunn said. "Have you seen her recently?"

"She was here two nights ago. Sat at the bar for some time before she left later that night. She looked upset," he replied. Some sweat dripped down his temple.

"Has she been working here?" Gunn asked.

"No, she has not. She never came back after the night before I met you," the clerk said.

"Thanks," Gunn said. He walked over to the saloon area. Behind the bar, he saw the same bartender from the night he had been there. The bartender looked at him. Gunn walked up to the bar and tipped his hat. It made him happy to hear she waited for him and that she had not returned to work. She deserved more than that life.

"You're bringing trouble with you," the bartender said.

Gunn said, "No trouble, I'll keep it molasses for you. Did the brandy come in yet?" He placed his rifle against the bar.

"It did yesterday," the bartender replied as he could sense this visit contained no malice. He took his hand off the shotgun under the bar and instead took a bottle and poured it into a glass for him. He put the glass in front of Gunn. Gunn grabbed it and took a drink.

"It is good," Gunn said. "Better than I thought it would be."

"Glad you like it," the bartender said as he took a glass as well.

"Aren't you supposed to sell it, not drink it?" Gunn replied.

"That is what my wife used to say. Sometimes you have to drink it before you can sell it," the bartender replied. Gunn laughed. They made conversation. The bartender cleaned the top of the bar. The gaming area was quite empty and practically silent.

The bartender was warmer than last time he had been here. Finally, the bartender asked him directly, "You made a stir last time you were here. That a habit of yours?" He leaned toward Gunn after he said it, testing him. "We don't take kindly to that type of behavior. Bad for business and all."

Gunn put down his glass. "Well, friend, we don't need to go making a mess." He put his rifle on the top of the bar with his right hand. He looked right into his eyes, into his soul, and said, "I'm not looking for trouble, but I ain't gonna let a son of a bitch harass a woman. Now, can I get another drink of that brandy?"

The bartender pulled back from Gunn. Gunn continued to stare at him. The bartender put the rag down and reached back under the bar. Gunn put his hand on the rifle. They stared at each other for a second. Gunn put his rifle down and leaned it against the bar. The bartender's eye blinked and his hand brought up the bottle of brandy and poured another drink. Gunn nodded at him.

"That roast was good that night," Gunn said. He took out the tobacco and rolling paper from his pocket.

"I will let the cook know," the bartender said.

Gunn rolled the cigarette and lit it. He took a puff, and the bartender looked at him. Gunn noticed this, and he took the cigarette out of his mouth and extended it toward the bartender.

"Have it, I'll roll another," Gunn said.

The bartender took the cigarette and smoked it. "Thank you," he said. Gunn rolled another for himself. They each smoked and continued to talk at the bar for some time. The bartender told Gunn some jokes, and the men laughed.

"You made quite an impression on Miss Corbett. She didn't come back after that night until two days ago. Sat right there for a time, almost like she was waiting on you."

"That is what I heard from the clerk," Gunn said.

"She sat there and got quite drunk on whiskey. Mighty disappointed you never showed up," the bartender said. "I don't know much, friend, but I do know disappointing a woman ain't a good thing."

"It ain't, and I am probably up shit's creek," Gunn said out loud. "Did she talk about her sister?"

"Aye, her sister left three days ago for Colorado," the bartender said.

Gunn took the last sip of brandy. "Where is her home?" he asked.

"It's about a three-mile ride west of town. Go west till you hit the field and then follow the stream. The road will split and go left. You will see the cottage on the hill."

"Thank you," Gunn said.

"Good luck," the bartender said. Gunn went to pay for the brandy. The bartender shook his head said it was on the house. He thanked him and took his rifle and went outside. He walked over to the stable and got his horse. It was half past three. He holstered his rifle and took off, following the directions of the bartender. His spur dug into the stomach of the horse with every kick. He reached the clearing. His throat tightened, and he felt anxious. He continued to the creek and followed it until he reached the fork. He went left. Soon, a cottage began to appear in the distance beyond some trees. There was a small barn and fenced stable. He slowed the horse as he got close. He pulled back on the reins hard and stopped the horse. He took the reins and tied them to the fence post near the barn.

He turned and walked toward the cottage. "Ora!" Gunn shouted. There was no answer. He took his first step onto the porch. He shouted again, "Is anyone here?" The board bowed with his weight. He swung the door open. The hinges creaked a little. He stepped inside the house and looked around. There was no one there. He looked around and saw how empty it looked and felt. There were potatoes on the stove and a bag that read Flour on it on a shelf in the kitchen. He saw a mirror on the one wall. He turned and went back outside. I missed her, he thought. His stomach sank for some reason, and he cursed himself. He turned and walked left and exited the door. He took out a cigar and lit it with a match. He took a puff. As he reached the edge of the porch, he looked to a path through the trees to the west. There was a gradual slope up this hill, and on it was a large elm tree. Under it he saw a figure sitting, looking out away from him. He began walking toward the person by the tree. He dropped his cigar into the grass. As he walked up the hill, he kept thinking, I hope it's her.

She was looking out toward the rolling hills and the river. Her hair was over her right shoulder. He was about twenty feet behind her to her right.

"What a view," he said in French.

Ora spun her head around with a look of joy and disbelief. She stared at him standing there. She smiled. "It is nice," she finally replied to him. The wind blew some of her hair into her face.

"I was talking about you," he said to her as he walked over to her. He crouched down and moved her hair from in front of her face to behind her ear.

She looked at him. "You trimmed your beard."

He replied that he did.

"You're quite the gentleman for standing me up," she said back to him.

"Desole," he said, "I got held up."

"You did? I am some fool to have waited for you to come back," she said like a dagger.

"Maybe you are. The bartender said you got drunk on whiskey," he said to dodge the hot knife she threw through the air.

"I did," she continued in French. "You would, too, if got stood up. Made to look like a fool waiting for a bastard."

"Bastard?" Everett said. "Last I checked parents were married when I was born."

She paused and then stopped. "That may be, but you're a bastard! Why did you come back?"

"I don't know," he replied. His shoulders eased, and his back didn't hurt. He smiled at her with a closed mouth. She sat back down and looked out over the hills again. She huffed and tapped the ground next to her. "I am glad you didn't leave."

"Glad you decided to show up," she said. "Isn't this view nice?" She changed the subject.

"It is something," he said to her, this time referencing the view. He looked at her face, and she looked back at his.

"It is. You are a gunfighter, aren't you?" she asked him with a rueful chuckle as they stared out onto the horizon. She looked at him with curiosity, and she turned toward him and studied his face as she waited for him to answer.

"Gunfighter?" He laughed out loud. "No, I'm a bastard." He paused and looked back over the hills. "A bastard that has the worst timing," he said with a smile.

She laughed and hit his shoulder. "Why did you leave the money?"

"The thought of your spirit breaking," he said to her seriously.

"It almost was," she said back to him.

"You didn't know if I would come back," he said to her.

"Something told me you would," she replied to him.

"Was it the whiskey speaking in your ear?" he said back to her.

"Fuck you," she said with a coy smile and slapped his arm. "Really, are you an outlaw?"

"I'm like a Pinkerton," he lied. "Nothing more than that."

"Is it dangerous, Everett?" she asked him.

"Only when you let your guard down. These help a lot." He tapped the guns on his hip. He liked how she said his name. No one had called him that for some time.

"How does it make you feel?" she asked him.

"Makes me feel terrible," he said back to her honestly. "Hell, I always feel terrible, but if I don't do it, someone else will, so I might as well earn a living."

"Why do it then if it makes you feel terrible?" she asked.

"Never could stick with anything else," he said. "I always had a gift."

"So"—she paused—"are you living or surviving?" she asked him.

"Surviving," he said back. This question penetrated him, and he felt ashamed. "What is the difference?" he inquired in French. He put his hand up to his face and studied her.

"Hope," she said. "I think surviving is just like dying, only really drawn out."

The comment shot through Everett like a bullet. He felt his heart drop for a moment. "I'm just surviving."

"Me too," she replied as she looked at him. He sat next to her under the elm tree, staring into the distance. "I want that to change," she said.

He sat silently and continued listening to her. "Dreams are a funny thing," he said. "Seems like you had a chance the other day," he said.

"I did, but I was gonna run away from here and be the same," she said to him.

"I know how that is," he said to her.

"I mean I don't even know you, and I waited for a stranger," she said. She thought she sounded crazy and felt embarrassed as he sat there next to her. "It is just that . . ."

"You saw hope and a way out," he said to her. She sat silent as he read her emotions. "I don't think you're crazy for staying. Just as much as I ain't crazy for coming back."

She listened to him. "Where will you go next?"

"The hotel," he said with a laugh.

"No really, where will you go next?" she asked him.

"Where I need to be, but west," he said to her very assuredly.

"I bet it's nice there," she said.

"Maybe you will find out one day," he said to her.

Chapter 10

They made dinner together that night in the kitchen, but she insisted he not stay with her that night. It made their conversation easier, and each could tell that they were letting down their guard. He had wanted to stay but listened to her and took his horse back to the town. He arrived late and went up to his room and went to sleep. He awoke in his bed at the saloon. He wrung his feet onto his bed and whistled while he put his pants and boots on. He rubbed the back of his neck with his hand after his boots were on. He put his shirt on and then his guns and grabbed his jacket but left his Winchester in the room.

He made his way to the bar and greeted the bartender. Both said good morning and left it at that. A storm was approaching and would arrive later in the day, the bartender told him. Gunn could feel it from his back and his ankle. The air felt heavy. Gunn ordered a coffee with a snake bite in it. He drank it down and then ordered another, this time without the snake bite.

"There is news of some silver mining north from Arizona and New Mexico in the territory," the bartender said.

"Silver, it'll almost be like California," Gunn said back.

"Should bring a lotta business through here," the bartender said. "Have to put up some wallpaper, bring some class to this place. Be great if we had the Pacific on our heels too. I'd love to see it one day."

"Sure would," Gunn said as he looked around at the barren walls. There was a picture of a sunset on the wall beyond the gaming tables he hadn't noticed before. They were so empty this day. "That Pacific, it would fill up the seats at all times of day."

"It would," the bartender remarked, "but that is for another day. Did you find Miss Corbett?"

"I did," Everett said.

"Was she friendly, or did she hold it against you?" the bartender asked.

"Friendly but held it against me. I apologized," Gunn said back.

"That is new for you, I imagine," the bartender said with a laugh, and he turned away from Gunn and cleaned some glasses with his rag.

"It is," Gunn said with a laugh. "I don't like it."

"Women do that to us," the bartender said to him. He turned and poured a beer for him. He swiped away the head of the beer with a stick and placed it in front of him.

"Thank you. How long have you owned this place?" Gunn asked.

"Oh, long time. I moved here with my wife after the war. We used her inheritance to open it. She cooked, I cleaned." He smiled and paused as Gunn laughed. "She got sick a few years later and fought it hard. Damn cancer."

"I am sorry," Gunn said. "Sounds like she was a good woman."

"She was, brightened many of my days," the bartender said to him. "Business is steady though."

"Sure is," Gunn replied to him.

"Did you ever get domesticated?" the bartender asked.

"Worked as a miller for a time." He took a sip of the beer. It was fresh on his lips, and the foam was on his beard. "About as settled as I ever got." He paused for a moment and took another drink.

"You ought to go see on Miss Corbett," the bartender said. "Might do you some good, getting domesticated. Tends to raise life expectancy."

"The rain's coming. I best be going that way. What do I owe you?" Gunn asked.

"Still on the house," the bartender said.

"Much obliged. One of these days, I am gonna have to pay you that tab, maybe before you ride on out to the Pacific," Gunn said and tipped his cap as he left the bar. He walked into the street and could see the storm clouds coming close, so he hurried to the stable. He paid the boy and took his horse and his rifle with him and rode to Ora's. He had to hurry to beat the storm. Again, he reached the clearing, the stream, and then the fork. He went left and soon saw the cottage in the distance. His mind was empty as the road. He came up to the cottage, and he slowed.

As his horse trotted, he heard a man yelling at her inside the house, and she was yelling back at him. He could hear it from outside the cottage. He dismounted from his horse and did not tie the reins up of his horse. The shouting continued, and he walked toward the house through the tall grass. As he came near the porch, the shouting stopped suddenly, and he heard crying. There was a white heat that crept up the back of his head down from his, neck and he clenched his teeth. He lowered his left hand to his side and grabbed the gun from his holster but didn't remove it. The metal pulled his hand like a magnet.

Through the front door, Ora crashed out onto the porch. She was on her hands and knees as she fell onto the planks. There was a red mark forming on the side of her face that was fresh, and there were tears running down her face. She was wiping them away with her left hand because her right arm stretched to keep herself up. She looked up and saw Everett. She saw this mad look in his eye that she recognized from the saloon from the night they met. It was the look of a rabid animal.

A man followed through the door out onto the porch. The man was about ten to fifteen years older than Everett and had black hair with gray sprinkled in. Once on the porch, the man raised a belt in his hand to hit her. "You good for nothing—" A gunshot rang out. The bullet hit the top of the door-frame above his head. Splinters shot out from the wood frame. Ora screamed out loud. Gunn had missed him on purpose but hit his mark on the door. The man dropped the belt as he said, "What the hell! What are you doing here, you son of a bitch?" He put his hands up like the coward he was.

Everett walked toward the man with the gun pointed right at him. He pulled back the hammer. Ora rolled over and began to crawl backward like a crab to give herself distance between them. The man stood in the doorway as Everett stepped onto the porch. His right eye twitched from anger. She was not able to speak, but her face became just had a blank scared stare.

"You've been beating her!" he screamed in a murderous rage with the gun pointed at the man. He stood there with the gun pointed at him.

"I smacked her around. She owes me money! She made money at the whorehouse. That bitch better give me my share."

"That bitch? Your share?" Gunn said as he tilted his head and looked over at Ora. "Let me give you what you're entitled to!" He shot at him near the leg to get him off balance as he stood in the doorway. The man fell down onto the floor and screamed in. Gunn held his pistol and knelt down and proceeded to punch the man repeatedly in the face with it. He punched him again and again until the man's face was bloody, but he was still breathing. Gunn took the gun and pointed it at the man's head and pulled the hammer back.

"Don't kill him!" she screamed. She came inside and grabbed Everett's face and turned it toward hers. "Please, he isn't worth it," she said in French. "He is still breathing, isn't he?"

"He'll live," Gunn said as he stood up and wiped the blood on his knuckles onto the man's pants. He got to one leg. His back tightened up on him, and he winced. Gunn crumpled to the ground.

"Are you okay?" Ora ran up to him as she screamed. She grabbed his shoulder and pulled him up.

"I'll be okay." He winced again. "Get your things. We are getting out of here. Does he have a gun?"

She looked down at James. "Give me a moment. He has a shotgun over the door," she said as she stepped over him lying knocked out on the floor in the doorway. She went into her room and gathered a few articles of clothing, the picture of her mother, and the cross on the wall. As she did that, Everett took the shotgun down from above the door and walked out to the barn. He threw the unloaded shotgun into the fenced pen. Gunn came back to the door and Ora waited there with a soft case with the belongings and put it up on his horse and tied it down. Ora walked to the barn and helped Ora prepared Maple for the ride. Gunn through the saddle over Maple and tied it down. He extended his hand to help Ora up the horse.

"I have it," she said to him playfully as she pulled herself up like a true professional. Gunn said nothing. He backed away, and she tried to mount the horse. She slipped and fell back onto her butt. Gunn stopped and opened both his palms to catch her.

"Big girl," he said with a laugh.

"Oh, shut up, can you help me up?" Ora said to him. Everett extended his hand and pulled her up. She put her first foot in the stirrup and pulled herself up as Everett pushed her. Everett watched her as she pulled on the reins and turned the horse toward Everett. "Well, come on then, let's go," she said.

Everett turned and walked over to his horse. He mounted it and found the reins. He kicked the horse and bolted off. Ora and Maple took off to him. Once they reached the clearing, Everett slowed, and Ora caught up next to him. The thunder started, and the clouds began to open up on them. The rain started slowly as a drizzle. "We should hurry before the storms opens up on us," Everett said to her.

"What am I doing?" Ora said to him.

"What do you mean?" Gunn said. "Riding off with me?"

"I am fool," Ora said.

Gunn laughed deep. "You would be a fool to stay."

"I can't just run off with a gunfighter," she said.

"Pinkerton, now come with me. We can visit your sister, and you can figure it out from there," he said.

"You would do that for me?" she said surprised.

"I would, but we have to travel like hell to get there," he said.

"All right, we have a few minutes. Let's go slow," she said to him as she looked at him. He looked taller, sitting on the horse in that moment.

Everett understood what she meant, and he slowed the horse. The field became damp as they rode back to the town. A slow drizzle began to fall. It felt good as it fell on his jacket. He tilted his head back and swallowed some of the rain. She looked at him and did the same. The rain began to fall faster and harder. The sky grew darker.

"I'm never coming back here," she said as she looked back toward the hills from which they came.

"I know," Everett said. "I don't want to either. I keep getting into fights."

"You do," Ora said to him. "Is Colorado nice?" she asked.

"I have never been," he said back.

"Good, it can be a surprise for us both," she replied to him.

They got into town and stabled the horses and went into the saloon. The water was running off their damp clothes onto the floor. The bartender was still there behind the bar. He had a cigar in his mouth, and he smiled showing his teeth when he saw them. He nodded at Everett to express his approval. Everett smiled and nodded back to him. The bartender waved them over to the bar. Everett led them through the crowd. He carried his rifle in his left hand and held Ora's hand in his right. The women in the establishment looked at her with jealousy and envy. Ora did not care what they thought.

"For you two, on the house," the bartender said as he placed two glasses of brandy on the bar. He took the brandy bottle, uncorked it, and poured it into the glasses.

"That's not necessary," Ora said. She wasn't embarrassed coming back to this place. She could care less. She took her hair and put it into a ponytail.

"Yes, it is," the bartender said. He poured a glass for himself. The three each took their glasses and toasted.

"I am paying for these," Everett said.

"Pay me tomorrow," the old man said to him. "Tonight, let's just enjoy a drink." Everett produced a small smile almost hidden behind his beard. He agreed. They all talked, and the room began to burst with laughter as everyone began to drink more and more. The night continued on. The gaming room became alive, and cigarette smoke blanketed the ceiling.

"I am going to bed," Ora said quite drunk and quite tired.

"I will walk you up," Everett said in French. Their conversation had slipped between English and French. When he couldn't remember the French word, he would curse with, and she laughed and told him what it was. They walked up toward his room. He pulled back the cover and helped her get into bed. She lay down, and he tucked her in.

"What a day," she said with her eyes closed and a smile.

"What a day," he said. He kissed her good night on the forehead.

"Won't you stay?" she asked as she lay on the bed.

"Soon," he said. "Get some rest."

"Good," she said as she fell asleep. He leaned over and kissed her forehead. "Thank you, Everett," she said. He said nothing. He made his way down the stairs and came back to the bar. Everett asked for a cigar and added this to his tab. He lit it and stood with a new brandy in his hand. He continued talking with the bartender and began playing a dice game for some time with another patron. When he felt tired, he asked the bartender for another brandy. His back ached.

"Quite a night cap, Everett," the bartender said. He poured another for both of them.

"No one calls me that except good friends," Gunn said.

"You don't have many of those, do you?" the bartender said.

"I don't, but lately I've been dealt spades," Gunn said. "What is your name?"

"Just seems to be myself and Miss Corbett," the bartender interrupted him. "Oh, and it's Joseph. But most people call me Wyatt."

"It is quite a pair. Why not call you Joe?" Gunn asked.

"I never figured that out. I think it was so my mom could remember which rancher my daddy was," Wyatt said. Both men laughed. The crowd had thinned out, and they were talking among themselves.

"Is that really why?" Everett said.

"No, it was a nickname after my pappy. But makes for a hell of a story," Wyatt said.

Everett laughed. "That makes a better story. I am drunk and need to go to bed. Good night, friend."

"Good night, friend," Wyatt said. Everett went upstairs. He took off his boots and crawled into the chair across the bed from Ora and stretched his legs onto the bed. He fell asleep with little effort.

Chapter 11

The wind tore across the prairie, seemingly pulling the grass out of the dirt. The branches of trees, weeds and grasses, and the flowers all leaned from the force of the wind. The wind tugged on their faces from the left to the right. Everett had put on an extra layer, and so had Ora. They rode side by side as he shielded her as best he could from the wind. It was later in the afternoon. They would not be reaching the town and would need to make camp soon. They had been on the road for nearly three weeks since crossing the Mississippi River. The air felt cold and heavy on their skin. The kind of weight signaling a powerful rainstorm was not far off. Everett looked to his left and could see in the distance the storm that in fact approached.

"It's gaining ground. After we make this hill, we are going to make camp. How are you holding up?" he asked her.

"I am cold. I can hold out until we have to stop," she answered him. Her cheeks were white from the air. He felt guilty seeing her shiver.

"Just a little longer. You handle yourself well?" he asked her.

"On the farm as children, we would camp out. Always near the house. It always seems to keep raining whenever we are together," she said rhetorically to him with a laugh.

He thought the same thing himself. He knew he would have to be patient as best he could. They needed to dig ditch around their camp to prevent mud and water from coming in on them, and he needed to put the tarp up as well. Then a fire needed to be made. It wouldn't take as long, but he would need to do most of it and his back ached. They continued, and they reached the clearing after the hill just off a thicket of trees. The land didn't seem to slope enough to have water run into their camp.

"Here is where we'll camp," he said. He stopped his horse and dismounted. She stopped her horse and looked around.

"All right, the clouds are getting damn close," she said with apprehension.

"We'll be all right," he said to her as he dismounted. He took her hand and helped her dismount. She looked back at them. He snapped his fingers. "Ora, it is fine. We have time. I need your help."

"What would you like me to do?" she asked him with her attention on him.

"I need you to tie your horse over to that short tree over there and then come back and do the same to mine," he said calmly.

"Okay," she said to him. She took Maple and walked her over to the tree and then tied the reins. The wind blew hard, and she held her hat on her head with her free hand. There was plenty of grass for the horse to eat. She walked back and took Everett's horse by the reins. He had unloaded several items from the horse while she had tied up Maple. He placed a small shovel, a tarp, the sleeping blankets, and the saddlebags on the ground. He searched for sticks to use as poles for the tarp to help block the rain in the tree and thicket. He came out with four strong sticks.

He used the shovel to hammer the sticks into ground with the blade. Each thud drove the stick further into the dirt. She watched for a second longer before saying, "Everett, what should I do next?"

"Take your belongings off your horse that you don't want to get wet," he replied. He turned and looked toward her. "After that, gather some kindling for a fire."

Ora went over to Maple. She unhitched her other bag and saddle and slid the saddle off the horse. She walked over and dropped the saddle next to Everett. It made a loud noise and startled him. She did this on purpose and wanted to let him know he didn't need to baby her. She had grit. She brought over her blanket and clothes from the horse. He had just finished tying up the tarp that was about three feet high. He kneeled and shoveled a ditch around the tent.

"Why are you doing that?" she asked him.

"It is to have the water flow around us and keep us dry," he replied. He had almost completed the trench, but suddenly he winced in pain and fell over. She knelt down next to him.

"What's wrong?" she asked him.

"Nothing," he said with a grimace. His forehead wrinkled.

"It's not nothing," she said back to him. "It has happened twice now."

"It is just my back. It will go away in a little while." He lay there under the tarp.

"When did you hurt your back?" she asked him. She sat next to him.

"Long time ago, damn thing still gives me trouble," he said lying on his back, looking up at her. He pointed to a spot in low back. He had rolled up his sleeves, and she saw a scare on his left arm.

"You're falling apart," she said. She pointed to the scar on his left arm about a foot long. "Let me look at it," she said.

"Some days it feels like it," he said as he lifted up his shirt. He pointed to a scar she had noticed on his arm. "They are both from logging. I got out of the way soon enough before a giant pine crushed me," he asked. "You didn't notice it at the hotel."

"You had your jacket on," she said to him coyly. "Where were you a logger?"

"In Ohio and Kentucky. I couldn't have been more than fifteen."

"How long did you do it?" she asked.

"I think about seven years and then started working as a ranch hand," he said.

His face eased as the pain stopped shooting and became dull. She was crouched next to him. "Ora, the firewood."

"Hold on," she said. "The discs in your back are injured."

"What the hell is that, and where did you learn that?" he said, looking perplexed.

"I know a lot of things," she said.

"Thank you, Doctor," he said to her. "How did you learn that?"

"It's your fourth or fifth that is damaged. I was the bookkeeper for the doctor. He taught me some, and I read the books."

"I am impressed. But, Ora, the firewood," he said. "You are something else. Damn near a doctor, at least a nurse."

"Oh yes, thanks for reminding me. I am something like that," she said. She went over to the thicket and collected some twigs and small sticks. Everett thanked her. He took out a flint stick from his pocket and his knife. He handed it to her, still grimacing slightly. She looked unsure of herself. He nodded and told her she had it. The first spark startled her, but the dry leaves and twigs started right up after a few tries.

"When you were a logger, you were taking orders for a change. Must have been hard," she said to him playfully. The light cast shadows on their faces.

"I did," Everett said to her. "Most of them didn't know their ass from a hole in the ground." They both laughed. He paused for a moment. He changed the subject by saying, "My hand is still bruised from punching your fella in the face." He showed her his fist.

She laughed. "My fella, oh please! I am glad you did. He had it coming for a long time." The thunder rolled in the distance. "Is your back feeling better?"

He tried to sit up and winced again. "I just need another minute," he said. "I am glad he wasn't your fella. He's too old for yah."

"He never laid a hand on me like that," he said. Ora turned the subject back to from what it had been changed from. "Why did you sleep in the chair both nights we were together?"

His face turned red. He tried to speak, but nothing came out.

"You can tell me," she said softly. There was still thunder in the distance.

"I ain't good at that sort of thing," he said to her. There was a tension in his face that she noticed. His breathing changed, and he broke off the openness between.

She sat looking at him, studying the wrinkles around his eyes and how his beard tied into his jaw and neck. There was only honesty in face and his words. She took his hand and said, "Well, get good at it. I ain't gonna hurt you, Everett."

"I didn't say I am scared of being hurt," he said. The tension remained in his chest.

"You didn't have to," she said back to him.

This frustrated Everett because he did feel that way and couldn't express it. She read him. "Besides, why you come back for me then and whisk me off that ranch?" she asked him faintly. "For the conversation?"

"You're making me regret taking you with me right now," he said, embarrassed.

"Oh stop," she said back.

"Before I saw you in the saloon, I saw you from the street with that blue dress on, and your hair was curled. Then when I heard you speak French—and I haven't heard anyone speak French for about six years—I had to come back," he said back to her. Some of that was a lie, but it was the truth.

"So it was for the conversation," she said back playfully.

"Something like that.," he said.

"Is your back better?" she asked. She smiled. She knew that this man cared for her.

He sat up. "It'll hold up. Thank you." He got to his knees and then began building the fire bigger at the base of the taller end of the tarp, placing the sticks in the best way to keep them warm. She watched his as he continued this for a few minutes. A small fire grew as he expected it to. The air had cooled some more and felt damp.

He stood up and gingerly walked over to the horse and dug a small ditch to allow water to collect for them. He had a slight limp at this point. He left the shovel near the horses. He walked back to the tarp. He lay down underneath it. She had spread out her blanket and sleeping mat on the ground. The rain was closer now but not overly hard.

"Do you have anything to eat?" she asked him.

"I just have some jerky and a can of pickled carrots." He took out the jar and bag of jerky.

She took a bite of the jerky and then opened the container of carrots. "I haven't had pickled carrots before," she said in between bites.

"You're not missing much. I grabbed this jar on accident," he said to her. He took the jar and took a bite of the carrots. He took out his steel flask and unscrewed the top. He took a drink.

"What's in that?" she asked.

"Brandy," he said. "Here have some." He handed her the flask. She felt warmer after taking a drink. She handed it back to him.

"This is life of a cowboy. It is pretty thrilling," she said sarcastically.

"It ain't thrilling. We are just missing the biscuits and beans," he said with a laugh. The rain was closer now, and so was the thunder. "What was life on the ranch like?" he asked.

"It was simple for a long time after my parents passed away." A loud bolt of lightning hit nearby. Ora grabbed Everett's arm. He held her close.

"Tell me about your parents," he said.

Ora was stunned. No one had asked her about her parents in such a long time. She had to pause because it caught her off guard and had to think of how to describe them. "Well, my mother was a strong woman. She taught us to speak French because that was something her mother did from her family. We went to school through third grade. My father, he died when I was eight. He caught the fever. From what I remember, he was a quiet man. He would sit on the porch on Sundays and tell us stories to put us to bed. My mom always smiled when she spoke about him."

"What happened to your mother?"

"She died a few years later. She went to sleep and never woke up," she said. "If she hadn't have helped me growing up, I wouldn't have gotten the job at the doc's office. He let me write his correspondence. I learned to read, to write, and some Latin."

"Speak some to more me," he said.

"Say please first," she said back.

"Si'l vous plait," he said to her.

"Causa latet vis est notissima," she said back to him.

"That doesn't make much sense. What does it mean?" he said with a smile.

"The cause is hidden, the results well known," she said. "A motto from his wall at the office. He was in a fraternity at his university." They were so enthralled with their conversation that they hadn't noticed it had started raining. It was not the hard rain they expected but a misty drizzle.

"What's a fraternity?" he asked.

"He told me it is a brotherhood that drinks lots of ale. That's all he told me," she said. The thunder and rain intensified. Ora ate another bit of carrot.

"The worst of it won't be through us for a bit," he said. Ora snuggled closer to him; he held her close. They shared a blanket.

"What do we do now?" she asked.

"We wait for the storm to pass," he said to her as he put his hat over his eyes and tried to sleep.

"How can you sleep?" she said.

"Years of practice. I am just resting my eyes. Just keep talking," he said back with his hat over his head.

She laughed. "For such a rugged man, you have a soft heart, Everett."

"Don't dog me," he said to her from under his hat.

"I am not dogging you. You aren't want I expected," she said back.

"What did you expect?" he said softer to her, almost falling asleep.

"Not a gentleman. You are deeper than you let on," she said with a yawn.

"Time may prove you wrong," he said with a yawn as he started to nod off.

"Everett, don't fall asleep, please," she said. He didn't respond and continued to snore. She took the butt of his rifle and poked him in the ribs. He grunted but did not wake up. She tried it again. "Wake up."

He picked his head up. "Oui."

"Stay awake during the storm at least," she said.

"All right," he said. They stayed dry under the tarp. The rain had begun to fall with more power. The water began to drain in the ditch that he had dug around them to keep them dry. They sat there and watched the fire for some time. They drank some more of the brandy and drank water from their canteens. There was lighting in the distance. It had grown very dark as night crept in. The rain had let up to just a light drizzle. They could hear coyotes in the distance. It could have been wolves, they were not sure.

After some time, she broke the silence. "It is beautiful out here."

"It is tonight," he said.

"What did you think of me?" she asked.

"I thought you were stubborn but strong," he said and after a pause added, "a little naive."

"Naive!" she said with a snort. "You couldn't be more wrong."

"I was right about you being stubborn though," he said back to her.

That comment meant a lot to her. "I am. I just never had anyone to lean on, and it made me well self-reliant. You know, I was almost married once. The guy ran off with some older lady. I think it made me stronger."

"It has," he replied as he listened to her words intently. The fire brought light to all their faces.

Ora interjected, "That is the worst kind of pain."

"It is," he said. "Nothing sets that right, not even time."

"Everett, just tell me straight, and don't lie to me."

"I ain't a coward," he asked her, and he turned to look at her.

"Just don't lie to me, promise me that," she said. He didn't reply to her and just stared into her eyes. The fire flicked in the reflection in her eyes.

"I promise," he said. "I will get you to Colorado."

"I know, but you can open up to me. It's all right," she said.

"I may not. It tears a man down to nothing."

"I would rather live a life that tore me down than one that kept me steady and unfulfilled," she said back.

"Why would you want that?" he asked back.

"I would know how strong I am and can appreciate the things that are really good in my life. That is something. I'll take something over nothing any day," she said to him. The thunder crept a little closer. And they could hear rain in the distance. "You should try not living with walls."

Everett sat there and looked at her for a several moments and then looked at the fire. The words she said drowned out the storm outside, and he felt the calming of the storm inside as well. This is something, he thought to himself. He took the last sip of brandy from the flask, and he put firewood on the fire. He wanted to change the subject.

"You get awful quiet," she said.

"Maybe, I was feeling something," he said back to her. He turned to his side and began to fall asleep. Ora soon fell asleep too. There they lay under the stars. They woke in the morning and packed their things. Neither spoke much to the other; they didn't have to. As they headed west, Everett angled them more north toward Colorado. If he squinted, he could almost see the giant mountains rise in the distance.

Chapter 12

The horse's hooves made noise as they moved over the stone-filled riverbank. They had been moving along a small river for some time. The water ripples on the top of the water moved like an improvised ballet. The tall pine trees created shadows on the ground that allowed each of them to not have to squint.

"How much further is it?" Ora asked him.

"We should be there within an hour," Everett replied. He turned back to see how Ora was handling her horse. She let it make slow deliberate steps to not injure the horse. She had made the decision to wear pants instead of dresses while they were out on the trail. She had gotten quite good, and they had been able to cover greater distances. They had flown through Kansas and Missouri. She had bought a cowboy hat to protect her face near Kansas City. "Your sister will hardly recognize you," he told her.

"She will have herself a laugh. I may hardly recognize her," she said proudly. She kicked Maple to gallop up next to Everett. Everett's head turned toward her. She leaned over and kissed Everett.

He smiled and said to her, "I am looking forward to meeting her."

"She will be hard on you at first, then ease up," Ora replied.

"I can handle that. What do you think will be for supper?" he asked.

"I don't know. I hope it's something warm. Three days of stale cornbread and jerky has been rough."

"It has. You should show her you learned how to shoot," he said.

"One thing at a time. I can't let her know that I lost all of myself on the ride out here," she said.

"You mean trading your dress in for pants," he replied. He felt easy, and his work and the calling of the metal on his hip had been absent for a few weeks.

"Something like that," she said back to him. He laughed at her. "Don't go laughing too hard. I could fire in your direction one of these days."

"A few weeks ago, I'd have been alright with that," he replied.

"Then my aim got good," she said with a laugh.

They continued on along the river until the bend that went around the large rock in the middle. The land surveyor at the bank told them this back in the town in the early afternoon. The plot of land her sister and husband owned was about a ten-mile ride along the river to the west. They would go higher into the hills to the near base of the mountain. Everett had purchased a double-barrel shotgun and shells because of the risk of bear attack. The shotgun was a Beretta knockoff that had a handle made of walnut and was not prone to misfire. He wasn't going to risk running in a grizzly out here and picked this gun because of its reliability. He had slung his regular repeater over his shoulder with a piece of rope to allow for the shotgun to sit in the rifle holster.

They followed left, away from the large granite rock. The cracks looked like veins from the earth, giving a heartbeat to the massive rock. Everett stared at the massive size of the boulder as they passed it. The stream began to travel faster as it got narrower. There was some brush that shrank the size of the bank, and the horses had to walk into the water as they continued on ahead. From behind a group of trees, there emerged a clearing and the makings of a cabin.

It was a good-sized cabin. The openings between the trees had been filled in with grasses and mud to keep it closed from the elements. The roof had a good pitch to it, and there were even metal hinges on the door. It looked rough and open in many places.

"They must have paid a pretty penny for those hinges," Everett said.

"Must have," Ora said. "Hello, Loren . . . Samuel . . . It's Ora," she cried out. There was no reply. Silence continued for several seconds, nothing but the sound of the stream running behind them. In the distance, they could hear the sound of an eagle screeching in the sky. Ora called out again. There was a sound from behind the door inside the cabin. Everett lifted the shotgun and pointed it at the door out of instinct. The door swung open.

"Ora?" he said. "It's so good to hear your voice."

Ora got off her horse, and she ran up to him and gave him a hug.

Samuel looked at Everett. He had lowered the shotgun. "Hello, nice to meet you."

Ora said, "Samuel, this is Everett. He is my—"

Samuel interrupted her, "Better half, I imagine. Glad you rode out here with her. I knew there was something keeping her back in Ohio."

"He is just a guide that led me out here," she finished while she blushed.

Everett got off his horse and walked up to Samuel. "Hello, I have to agree with you. I am definitely her better half." Ora hit his arm. He reached out and shook Samuel's hand. It was weak and frail.

"Where is Loren?" Ora asked him.

"She is out back. Why don't you come inside?" Samuel said. "Everett, I'll help you with the horses."

"Sounds good," Everett said. He and Samuel led the horses over to the lean-to that had been constructed on the other side of the house. Most of it was made of rocks, sod, and fallen tree branches. They tied the horses next to the two work mules.

Everett noticed the apprehension on Samuel's face and could sense that something was amiss. "Everett . . ." He paused before continuing, "Loren died on the way out here. She caught a type of fever and couldn't pull through." His eyes began to tear up, and his voice trembled. "I stopped outside Kansas City for two weeks and got a doctor. It didn't matter. I tried. I tried goddammit! She died and is buried in some patch of dirt back in Kansas."

Everett grabbed Samuel's shoulder with his right hand. "I'm sorry. Don't blame yourself for that." It is all he could say.

"I was supposed to take care of her!" he said hopelessly.

"You did all you could do. Stop acting like this," he said.

"You're right. I have some of her things inside in a chest," he said. "I should give 'em to Ora." They both walked around to the door and found that it hadn't closed. Ora was sitting on a chair next to the table. She had her elbows on the table and was holding her hands to her face as she was sobbing into her hands. Samuel and Everett walked up to her, and each put their hand on her shoulder.

"I'm sorry Ora, she didn't make the trip. She got sick, and by the time we made it to a doctor, it was too late," he said.

"I heard you both talking out back," she said. She stood up and hugged Samuel. "I am sorry, Samuel," she said.

"I am too," he said back to her. Everett stood in silence. It wasn't his place to say anything he felt. "There are some of her things in the chest over by the stove. Just a necklace, a dress, a picture, and a locket. I want you to have them," Samuel said to her.

Ora looked at him and asked, "Are you sure?"

"Yes, I can't carry them with me," he said. Samuel stood up and walked over to the chest. He opened it and took out the articles and handed them to her. Tears filled his eyes and her eyes.

"How are you handling this mess?" Ora said as she took them from him

"It's been hard," Samuel said. "I can make a go of this yet though."

"I will make supper for us," Ora said.

"I would appreciate that, but I have no food, Ora," Samuel said; he sounded defeated. It was then they realized how hard it had been on him. He stood like a broken man. Ora noticed how pale and weak he looked now. She hadn't noticed it before. She looked quick at Everett. He looked back at Ora.

"Samuel, grab your coat. We are going to town for food tonight," Everett said.

"I couldn't ask you to do that," Samuel said.

"I didn't ask, I insist. Grab your coat so we can make the kitchen," Everett said. Samuel looked at Everett. It was a look of gratitude and respect. His eyes said it without him having to. The gesture of kindness and sympathy from man to man humbled the other. He went and put on his coat while Everett and Ora waited outside. Each had gotten their horse and placed the saddle on both of them. Samuel walked over and untied his horse. He had no saddle and threw a blanket over the top of the horse's back. The horse grunted, and he turned the horse around. Samuel went in front of Everett and Ora. It took them a good hour, but they reached the town. The skies were clear, and the sun had begun to set. They tied their horses to the post outside the restaurant.

"Go on inside. I will meet you in moment," Everett said. Ora and Samuel nodded and went into the café. They grabbed a table half way to the back along the wall. Everett walked into the store next to the café. It was a goods store. The clerk behind the counter was a round man. He had white and reddish hair.

"What can I do for you, sir?" the clerk said.

"Do you have any saddles?" Everett asked.

"I have a used one right here," the clerk said and picked it up onto the counter. "That will be twenty dollars."

Everett took the money out of his saddlebag that he had carried with him. He laid the money on the counter. He thanked the clerk, and the clerk thanked him for the business. Everett carried the saddle outside. His lower back hurt him, and the pain shot down his left leg, causing him to limp. He hoisted the saddle over Samuel's horse and buckled it underneath. There were no windows in the café, and Samuel would have no idea. Everett could imagine what that felt like.

Everett opened the door. The bell rang above the door as it opened. The hostess looked up at him. There were people talking and smoke rising in the café. Some looked up to see who he was but then went back to their conversations. He saw Ora at a table along the wall. He did not see Samuel, and he walked over to her. She had taken off her hat and let her hair down.

She had tears in her eyes but kept breathing deeply, trying to hold them back. She smiled at him and grabbed his hand. Their travels had carried them far, but this was the first time he had supported her.

"How are—" he began to ask.

"Awful . . ." she said as she had tears fall down her face. "I feel awful for Samuel. I miss my sister."

"I am sorry. What was your sister like?" he asked in French. He continued to hold her hand as he sat across from her. She lightly squeezed his hand. He breathed and decided to let her vent. He forgot that the iron sat on his hip.

"She was just a loving and adventurous person that didn't let anything affect her mood, rain or shine," Ora said. "What a sister should be, I suppose."

"She sounds nice. I wish I could've met her," he said.

"She would've had you laughing," she said to him. She looked at him and squeezed his hand. She smiled.

"Now I wish I had met her. Where is Samuel?" he asked.

"He went to the outhouse," she said and then exhaled deeply. "He has run out of money and can't stay at the cottage," she said. Everett just looked at her. He coughed twice from the smoke in the air. He shifted his weight to his right hip to ease his back.

"That is dire straits," Everett said. "It's hard to come back from that. Are you going to stay with him here?" Everett asked. Strangely, this came out of his mouth, showing more emotion than he had wanted.

"I could try," she said. "I should try."

"It would be hard," Everett said. He suddenly realized he would miss her if she stayed.

"It would be," she asked him. He realized that they had not let go of each other's hands. He stared into her eyes and saw his own reflection. He didn't like what he saw. "It was just a thought," she said to him and pulled her hand away. She knew she wouldn't want to see Everett leave again.

He realized he hadn't replied to her yet and just kept staring. "It would be a good thing if you did stay." His heart ached as he said this.

She hadn't expected him to be so supportive of them separating. After the pause, she said with calm conviction, "I will manage both just fine if I do." She noticed the wrinkles under his eye. They continued to look at each other, and she began to notice the age in his eyes. A depth almost, she thought.

"What about Samuel?" he asked her to break their gaze at each other.

"Yes, where is he?" she asked and looked around. She said to him, embarrassed, "Could we help him at all get back on his feet?"

"Por vous, claro que si," he said in French. He had noticed how she used we in that sentence. It was his money, he thought to himself, but he had more than enough.

Ora finally let go of his hand again. She tilted her head and looked into his eyes and said, "Thank you." She saw her reflection and could see her eyes had dried. As they finished talking, Samuel walked back toward them. He sat and apologized to them for looking unkempt. The customers in the café began to laugh in the far corner at a crude joke about a priest and multiple naked women. Samuel laughed at this and cracked a smile; Everett and Ora laughed too. The tension seemed to ease, and the conversation began to flow. They ordered lagers and began to drink the beer. The waiter brought out bread and some chicken potato mash with beans and carrots. It smelled good and had a thick dark gravy on it. Samuel ate two plates. They had cherry pie afterward.

Samuel leaned back and put his hands on his stomach. "I can't move," he said.

Everett was leaning back and had a beer in his hand. He nodded in agreement. Ora laughed.

"I know, the ride back will be terrible," she said.

"Not happening," Everett said. Both Samuel and Ora looked at him, confused. "I am seeing two of you or three of you." Both of them laughed.

"Why three of me?" Ora asked. Everett looked away from her but tried to answer in her general direction. Both Samuel and Ora continued to laugh at him. "Okay, you are drunk. Let's walk out to the hotel and get two rooms."

"You are too generous. I can't accept this," Samuel said.

"Sam, shut up and help me carry him to the hotel," she said. The patrons watched as the girl in the pants and the scrawny man with the shaggy beard carried out the gunslinger by throwing his arms over their shoulders and dragging him out of the place. They kicked the door open of the café. The patrons applauded as they exited.

"I have to piss," Everett slurred as they carried him out.

"Dammit, help me get him to the alley," Ora said.

"I can manage on my own," Everett said. "Just need to undo my pants."

"I will get you out there," Samuel said. Everett nodded okay. Samuel dragged him to the alley and leaned him against the wall of the store. He faced away from the street and pulled his trousers down, and he began to pee. The sound of the stream hitting the ground made Samuel laugh. Everett had tears flowing down his face, but he held back sobbing. He wiped his eyes, and they stumbled back toward the rest of them.

"Is he always this much fun?" Samuel asked Ora.

"You have no idea," Ora said sarcastically. Everett stumbled back over to them, and his shirt was untucked. Together, they carried him over to the hotel. They walked in and set him on the chair in the lobby. They waved to the clerk and ordered two rooms. He had them write in the book and went in the back room to get the room keys.

"Ora, I haven't seen you this happy in a long time," Samuel said. "It's something good in a bad time."

"Thank you, Samuel. I am so sorry about Loren," Ora said. Both began to tear up.

"Thank you. She was an amazing woman," Samuel said. The clerk returned and gave them their keys. They thanked him.

"She was," she said. "Can you help me get him to the room?" Samuel nodded. They tipped Everett up and slid him down to the room. They used the key to open the door and lay him on the bed. The blanket was blue, and they tucked him underneath it. Ora walked back to the door. She hugged Samuel. They both said good night to each other. Then she said, "Samuel, I feel I should stay here with you."

"Ora, I appreciate that. I can't tell you what tonight meant for me, but you're not staying behind with me," Samuel said to her. "That life is over, and I am not gonna hold you back. You have a good thing with him."

"With Everett, we aren't . . ." she said, blushing.

"You're crazy about each other. Just admit it and run with it," Samuel said.

"I will. Everett and I wanted to give you some money to help get back on your feet," Ora said to him. "It isn't much." She took out three hundred dollars and gave it to him.

Samuel was shocked. He began to sob. Ora hugged him. She had never seen a grown man weep like this. He pulled back. "I'm some charity case, huh?"

"No, you're not," she said as she hugged him. "Good night, Samuel."

"Good night, Ora." He nodded. Ora hugged him again.

My sister was lucky to have you, she thought to herself. Ora turned back and went in the room. She heard Samuel's door close in the hallway. She lay down next to Everett. He was snoring. She didn't know it now, but Samuel would leave before them in the morning. She would never see him again but would think of him often and what his life had become. Samuel would work on a fishing boat in San Francisco and married a Dutch woman named Lyana. He named his daughter Loren. It was his token to carry on his first love throughout the world.

Ora lay in bed under the covers. Everett continued to snore. She kissed him on the cheek and then turned over. That was the first time she kissed him. There was a window, and the moonlight shone in. She stared at the night sky. A tear rolled down her cheek. She thought of Loren, the times they played as children. Her fingers gripped the blanket tighter. She laughed when the memories became funny. She stopped laughing and flipped her hair out of her face. Mostly tears fell off her face.

It was a cold evening, and the blanket was thick. Everett rolled over, and his arm fell over her. She remembered she had forgotten to take off his gun belt when she felt the holster poke her in the back. She was too tired to care. She said a prayer and finally fell asleep holding the locket in her hand.

The next morning, she finally woke him. He struggled to open his eyes. "Everett, Samuel rode out this morning," she said calmly, awaiting his reply.

He rubbed his eyes, and Ora repeated herself more anxiously. "I knew he would," he said. He sat up in the bed and grabbed his hat off the dresser next to the bed. "It'll be all right. Did I get that drunk?" he asked her.

"You were quite a mess, Everett. I haven't laughed that hard in a long time," she said, laughing.

"My second career as an entertainer is off to hell of a start than." He glanced around the room. He could feel her looking at him, gaging what he would say next. "I don't think you can go back to the homestead?" he asked her.

"He may still be there," she said but lying through her teeth.

"No, he ain't. I can leave you at the homestead," he said to gauge her reaction. Her smile evaporated.

"What do you mean you can't leave me here!" she shouted.

"What do you want then?" he asked her.

"You can't be that dense, can you?" she said rhetorically. She spun around to look at his reaction.

"Hardly," he said. "Ora, you can't go with me. Something would happen to you, and I couldn't—"

She cut him off, "Couldn't what, live with yourself? Abandoning me in middle of Colorado, that's better. Some man you are."

"Dammit, you know I am fond of you," Everett said in French. "You want to get caught up with an outlaw, have a life with me. One day I ain't gonna make it home, and it'll just be you."

"I'd rather have it that way," she said. "So what's the problem, Everett, you think I am gonna run off on you?" He stood silently, looking at her. She looked at him. "That is why you drank last night, because I was leaving." She walked over and kissed him. "I am not gonna run out on you, Everett."

He felt emotions and did his best to control himself. He held her there, and they fell back onto the bed. Sometime later, they dressed and left the motel. In the stable, Everett paid the fee. He hoisted and strapped both saddles on the horses. She watched him move. It seemed like perfect harmony with the universe. He looked at her, and the sun came in from the barn door behind her and made her features darker and more pronounced. She looked as beautiful as anything he had ever seen. They traveled back the path they came down south to New Mexico.

Chapter 13

They had traveled south for many weeks. They had stayed close to waterways and the Fremont cottonwoods decorated the valleys and pitches of the land that drew the water. The cactus sprouted up like flower buds across the open areas between the areas of grass. They had come upon a village and needed to trade for some food as their rations had run low. Both were hungry and had left behind much of their clothing from the north.

The air had grown dry and made traveling during the heat of the day difficult. Water had become their most valuable and scarce resource. He had purchased two additional canteens once they had reached a camp in southern Colorado. He thought how difficult the journey would have been without them as they had stopped to rest momentarily. He handed the leather-bound canteen to Ora who took a sip and handed it back to him. Her face was tanned from the sun, and she wore a wide brimmed leather hat and a cloth covering her face from the sun that she lowered to take a drink.

"I look like a regular frontier woman," she joked.

"You hold your own pretty well," he said as he took back the canteen from her and took a drink himself. He was glad she had been able to joke, it helped her mourn her sister. "Sure don't look like a lady from Ohio."

"It's the hat, isn't it," she said to him as she laughed and pulled the cloth back up over her face.

"It just might be," he said. He had watched these previous weeks, looking for habits and her reactions. He had marveled at her strength and positivity from her sister's death. Her mood had remained steady as she adapted quickly to this new life. He had worried she would become inconsolable while on the trail and it had been the opposite.

"Why are you looking at me like?" she asked him.

"I'm not sure what I am looking at." He thought about when he had killed a rattlesnake and shown her how to skin it and cook it.

"What do you mean?" she asked him.

"I thought I had you figured."

"Si tu pense," she said to him. She had brushed her hair back behind her ears. The sun continued to fall, and the sky had turned red and orange in the horizon on their left as they headed south.

"Looks like the mission is up ahead." He pointed with his right hand.

"Lead on Everett, let's catch it before dark,"

Everett took the reins and gave his horse a kick to get him moving. They had pushed on and had reached the New Mexico Border the day before. The land had become drier and flatter, but the brush remained abundant. About fifty miles back, they had ridden into a cattle drive party. They were familiar with the territory and had been helpful to them. While they shared some beans and cornbread with the them, the leader had mentioned something the cattle driver had told him that there would be mission on this trail. He wasn't lying, he said under his breathe. The temperature began to drop.

As they drew nearer, they saw a large structure emerge from open ground and it was surrounded by other homes made of clay bricks. Out past the structures, they could see a stream bank winding back and forth. He shook two of the canteens with his left hand, one was completely empty, and the other had run dangerously low. He looked back at Ora. She had wrapped herself in a blanket to stay warm. He looked back and could see people moving around the large structure.

They crossed the last stretch of dry, cracked earth and reached the settlement. There were a dozen or more homes around the mission. They could see the round ends of the wood beams protrude out from the tops of the walls. Some of them had been white washed with paint, and others had been left to have their natural color baked and harden by the sun. Smoke rose from several of them, and others had fires going out in front of the home. The sun had almost set when they met the people. The firelight brought them out of the shadow. Everett and Ora could see the faces of the people as they moved forward.

They were Native Americans, part of the Pueblo Indians, and were a friendly people. Some of the children waved at them, and the older people merely stared silently at them as they passed. They were focused on cooking their squash and beans over the fires in the street. The men continued talking in a tongue they did not understand but did not view them suspiciously.

To their surprise, there were Mexican families in the homes next to the Indians. Their children played with the Indian children. He saw these families preparing rice, beans, and tortillas for their supper. He heard them speaking Spanish and could not understand them.

"Hola Amigo," one of the men said to him.

"Hola, Amigo," he replied. Ora stayed behind him. He stopped his horse and stood silently. One of the Indian men walked over to the Spanish man, and they began to speak back and forth, and then turned back to Everett and Ora.

"Hablas Espanol, amigo?"

"No, amigo. No hablas Espanol."

"Si, Si, une momento,." The man shouted, "Charles Jones, trae tu trasero aquí."

A voice bellowed out from behind the homes. "Trae tu trasero aquí?"

"Solo levántate aquí, tenemos un visitante y él no habla español?"

"Espera, ¿es un gringo?

"El es."

"Be right there," the man said.

Everett and Ora looked at each other. Everett had placed his hand on his pistol as they had ridden up. He had kept it there the entire time. Everett breathed easy and soon the man called Charles Jones walked out from behind the pueblo and into view. First, they saw his boots and finally his face as he stood on the other side of the fire from them. He was a black man and wore denim pants, a wool jacket over a dark red shirt. He had a pistol belt on that he could see below the jacket. There was a cigar in the corner of his mouth.

Charles Jones said, "El es a gringo Pablo. So Gringo, you got a name for you and your partner there or does gringo got a nice ring to it?"

"Much as I enjoy the sound of that, doesn't sound too friendly."

"Friendly as you intend to make it."

Everett took his hand off his pistol. "Well Charles Jones, my given name is Everett, and this is Ora."

"Hello Gentleman," Ora said as she lowered the handkerchief from her face cutting off Everett. Pablo said hello to them in Spanish.

Everett didn't mind it and continued, "We don't intend to guff anybody. Just looking for a place to bed down for a few days." Everett got off his horse and hitched the horse to a post. He walked over to Charles Jones and Pablo. He extended his hand to each of them, and Ora dismounted and did the same.

Charles Jones turned to Pablo and translated back into Spanish for him what they had said. Pablo smiled at them and shook their hands. One of the men from the Indian group walked over to them and asked Pablo what was happening.

Pablo replied in Tiwa, "They are travelers, looking to sleep before continuing their journey."

Everett asked Charles Jones as they listened, "What are they saying?"

"I don't speak Tiwa. We have to get this second hand."

"You two are like two sides of the same coin." Ora said to him. The three of them laughed.

"What did he say?" Charles Jones asked Pablo in Spanish, and Pablo replied to him. Everett and Ora waited patiently to hear what he had said as they listened. Charles Jones turned to them and said, "He asked what the white men wanted, and Pablo said you wished to stay. He does not protest you staying."

"That is good, what is his name?" Everett asked him.

"His name is Hawk from Fire."

Hawk from Fire said to them, "Bepuwave."

Charles Jones said to them, "I know that one, it means welcome."

"Bepuwave," they said in return and shook his hand. His skin was worn, rough but had a surreal quality to it. He stood shorter than Everett but looked wise. He nodded and turned and walked back to his family.

"Are we able to stay in the church?" Everett asked Charles Jones.

"You mean the mission. Brother Pierre will have a say in that."

"Can you take us to him?" Ora said.

"Come this way," he replied and led them down the street towards the large building. They left the horses hitched in front of the homes. It stood two stories tall, perhaps thirty feet or so. The wood beams protruded out from the clay, and they looked like the pine from the trees they had seen in Colorado. No trees were this large where they were. There was a courtyard inside the walls to the right of the two-story section. Inside the court yard was a stable and inside of it was a well toward the center. They were lanterns and candles that illuminated through the windows of the mission. On a bench about thirty feet inside the gate was a man in a light gray tunic. The man sat silently facing away from them. Charles Jones led them up to the man. Pablo had followed them. They could see his face from the side in the lantern light. He had a longer beard that had turned gray, but some black hairs sprinkled it. His hair thinned, and he had large ears.

"Evening brother Pierre."

"Why hello Charles Jones. Hola Pablo. What a fine evening, Bueno noche."

"Fine evening," each replied. Ora and Everett stood behind them.

"And who are your friends behind you?"

"This is Everett and Ora. They are travelers and wanted to see if they could stay in the mission for a couple of days."

He turned and looked them up and down. Everett and Ora stepped forward. "Nice to meet you brother Pierre," they both said and shook his hand. His eyes studied them as he ran his hand through his beard and sat silently.

"Nice to meet you as well. You both are most welcome to stay as long as you need. I just hope you like tequila and mead. We have separate rooms for you both."

"I haven't had tequila," Ora said, "but mead will do just fine. Thank you."

"I'll drink whatever you have."

"Praise the Lord. Charles Jones, Pablo, why don't you both come back in a half hour. We will share some tequila and mead to bless the occasion."

"Sure thing brother," Charles Jones replied and translated back to Pablo. They turned and walked back towards their homes.

"I will get the horses," Everett said. He didn't want them checking his saddle bags, even though he kept the money bills inside his buttoned coat pocket.

"Please feel free to put them in our stable."

"Thank you," Everett said and turned back and walked into the darkness. He saw the horses hitched to the post where they had left them. He opened the saddle bags and saw that nothing had been moved. He looked up and saw Hawk of Fire looking at him. Everett stared back at him.

"You don't trust our people?" he said in English.

Everett stood shocked, "I was worried."

"You people, so quick to judge."

"I am sorry. I meant no offense by it."

"No offense taken Everett."

"Would you join us for tequila? The brother insists."

"I will join you,"

Everett took out two cigars from his saddle bag. "Cigar?"

Hawk of Fire took the cigar and smelled it. He put it in his mouth, "Good tobacco, thank you."

"Why didn't you say anything in English before?"

"Best to let others think the least of you I say."

"I like your style. That got you far?"

"It got me a cigar. I will see you soon."

Everett nodded and took the horses back up to the stable. He put them away and stored the saddles. He carried the things into the mission and met some of the other brothers.

***

Everett knew this area had grown with prospecting of gold and silver mining had peaked the interest in his conversations with Vernon. He had not shared this with Ora. For a moment, he thought of the rattlesnake they had eaten a week before. She had shot it, and he had shown her how to clean it. She named out some of the bones and organs as they separated parts of the animal. Everett sat in awe as she had spoken about many subjects. He smiled as he brought the horses back to the mission. The hooves clunked on the hard ground.

Soon he saw the mission, the light from lanterns revealing it in the distance. He passed a few large prickly pear cacti. To his left he saw two Pueblo men carrying with them a mule deer tied to a wood pole. It hung upside down as they carried it to the village. He could hear the families cheer with excitement as they would begin to clean the deer for dinner.

When he had reached twenty yards from the Mission's gate to open area with the stable, he saw fires out about a hundred yards from the mission. From the fires, he saw a makeshift shanty town. There were a few wagons, and here there were a few white settlers. They had pelts, grain, and pans scattered about. He could feel the cold on his hands as he led horses into the stable and took off the saddles and saddle bags. Around the fire, he saw Pierre, Ora, Charles Jones, and Pablo. He listened to them as they spoke to her as generous hosts. He put the horses away in the stable and brought the saddle bags with him.

Everett walked over and sat down next to him. Pablo handed him a glass of tequila. The round jug sat to the left of the table. They were all laughing together and warming themselves next to the fire pit. Everett set the belongings next to the bench and took the glass. He had only had tequila twice in his life. He took a long drink.

"Where have you all traveled from?" Pablo asked.

"Colorado," Everett said.

They laughed as he coughed from the tequila.

"You drink like a Baptist," Pierre said and they all laughed.

"You're funny for a man of God," Everett replied with a laugh. "This is potent."

Hawk with Fire approached and sat at the other of the pit. Everett looked past them and admired the mission. The church and living area had been built of mason bricks just as the Pueblo homes had but reinforced with larger timber brought south from the mountains to allow for a second story. There were several brothers all together, and they had greeted all of them.

Hawk with Fire took a drink after pouring a glass. He finished it quickly and poured another. He had the cigar that Everett had given him in the corner of his mouth. They all continued to tell stories and laugh. A different set of brothers brought out bowls of hot stew for them all to eat. The steam rose from the bowls.

Brother Pierre said, "Let us say grace." They all prayed.

The stew smelled good and they were unsure of the spices. Everett and Ora waited for the others to eat from the bowls and then grasped their spoons and took a bite. It was delicious.

Several hours passed like this until all returned to their homes and it grew quiet. "It is time to sleep, come this way." Pierre said. He led them over into the mess hall which was the large room on the right side of main hallway. They saw the large black pot with a stew inside of it.

"What was it made of?" Ora asked.

"It is a squash, bean, and chicken stew," he said. This eased their fears. Pierre put the cover on the kettle.

"Do you have any water?" Everett asked.

He nodded and brought a jug of water and two metal cups.

Everett thanked him and poured water into each cup. They stood in silence, but Ora heard one of the other brothers speaking in French in the corner.

"Is he speaking French?" she said to Everett.

His eyes perked up and replied, "He is, in this territory?"

Pierre leaned in and said in French, "He is, much to your surprise?"

"But how, in this part of the Spanish territory?"

"We are the last remaining French mission from the New Mexico Trail. More of a mix now of English, Spanish, Hopi, and French."

Everett and Ora looked around the room and saw the art on the walls. The words, written in French, stood out in candle light.

"You don't say. Doesn't seem like they have helped you out much by the looks of things," Everett said as he saw the damage to the foundation and general degrading of the building.

"Our brothers at the Spanish missions still hold on to that rivalry. It is best to let them win. We just do our best to serve."

They continued talking about the history for an hour. Ora had gone in and went to sleep.

"Are you looking to stay permanently in the area?" Pierre asked.

"I wouldn't be opposed," Everett said.

"Take a look at cabins about three miles east of here. Old ranchers had built them but moved on. Everyone here prefers the village."

"I will do that Pierre."

"Good. Well I will get some rest. Good night and God Bless."

"Toi aussi. Bon nuit," he said back.

Everett walked Ora to the room and made sure she fell asleep. He went back outside and stayed out by the fire watching the flames. He stared at it in silence. Hawk with Fire returned and sat across from him and studied him. Neither man spoke.

"The cigar was good."

"Glad you enjoyed it."

"There is conflict inside of you," Hawk with Fire said. "It has been there a long time."

"You observe a lot. Long time is right."

"Conflict exists in all of us. Peace is found through time. There will come a time where you will see a hawk in the sky, you may be released."

Everett confused said, "I'll be looking for that."

Everett continued to talk with Hawk with Fire. He soon realized he sat in the presence of a wise man. The sun began to rise and Everett realized he never fell asleep.

Chapter 14

It had been several months since that day in Colorado. Each had taken to the other, and besides their own stubbornness at times, causing momentary discord, they both found something they had not found with each other's companionship. Everett had left several times for his work and had returned unharmed. Ora never questioned this but worried about in silence if his gun belt returned with fewer cartridges on it. They had found a nice cabin and land he bought near the mission. Then one night, a mountain lion walked onto their purchase and scratched the door during dinner. It begged for some of the food it smelled inside. There was a nice pelt that hung over the fireplace since that day.

On this day, Ora sat on the rough oak table. She had a glass of wine next to her as she cut up the vegetables for dinner. The sun was not starting to set. Everett walked inside and put his hand on top of her hand that was holding the knife. "Relax, let me help you with that," he said and then kissed her. She smiled at him. He began to slice the vegetables as she sat next to him, drinking her wine. He looked at her, and she looked at him.

"I am glad I met you," he said to her.

"Oh, well, I am, too, or I would have been freezing in Colorado," she said back with a laugh. "That is the wine talking. I am sorry." They continued speaking French.

"No, keep going," he said to her. He just liked to listen to her talk. He continued dicing the vegetables.

"Only the ones with you," she said and kissed his cheek. "It was terrible you were late coming back to the town. I felt so foolish."

"I almost killed my horse to get back," he said back. He scooped the vegetables into a pan and stood up and walked over to the fire in the fireplace. The lamb leg roasted over the fire, and he began turning it a quarter turn to cook it evenly. He took the fire clamper and took a log and placed it in the oven to help start the kindling. He walked back to the table and took the pan with the vegetables. He placed it on the iron stove. He put his hand over the top of the stove and began to feel the heat.

"Maybe you should have," she said with a laugh.

"I ask him that sometimes. 'Why didn't you just fall over?'" he said back. "He never answers me." She laughed at him. He took some of the butter and threw it in the pan. "We have too much fun."

"We do," she said. "Everett, these past few months have been wonderful. Thank you."

He looked over at her as she sat on the table. She had on a long tan-and-white dress. Her hair was pulled back. He stared in silence. The light from the fire reflected off her eyes. She smiled at him. It was a smile he had grown to love. It was an honest smile that bared her soul. It was part mischievous, part playful and caring, but always reserved. What Everett loved most was her reserved nature. She was stronger than he was inside. Nothing would or could dampen her spirit because it shone too bright.

The lard in the pan began to sizzle. He took a wood spoon and stirred the vegetables. Next, he turned his attention to the lamb leg. He turned it again. The meat was beginning to marble, and the grizzle dripped off it into the fire. She watched him as his back was toward her, tending the meat. He moved gracefully despite his back pain. There was an elegance his movements that showed a refinement; it came from his ability to do things in the fewest ways possible. His speech was rough and short. He had trouble with some of his French, and this made her laugh. There was a wildness to him that she could see in his eyes that remained unexplained. His long hair was tucked back behind his ears.

He carved pieces of the leg with a knife and fork. He put the strips onto a plate for her and himself. He took the vegetables with a spoon and put them on each fork. There was some hard tack, and he placed it on each plate. He brought it back to the table. She had taken a seat on the bench, and he placed her plate in front of her. He sat across the table from her. They looked at each other.

"This is good wine," she said. "Would you like some?"

"Please," he said back to her. She poured him some from the bottle. She set the bottle down and then looked back at Everett. They had bought a case of this red wine at a saloon about a month ago. He kept it cool in the cellar. He carried it out for her, and she remembered how, for the first time in her life, everyone had their eyes on her. She enjoyed that feeling, but a strange humility came over her as well.

After they said grace, they said, "Bon appétit," and began to eat. The lamb leg was tender, and the vegetables fulfilled their purpose. The hard tack needed to be eaten and gave no particular flavor to the meal. The wine, however, went nicely with it all.

"How is it?" he asked her with a smile.

She finished her bite of lamb. "Wonderful, it is wonderful. What man around these parts cooks for their woman? I can't think of one." She wiped her face with a napkin.

"Only for rare occasions," he continued in French. They both finished their meal.

"What celebration?" she asked him. Her eyes widened with excitement. She sat up in her chair.

"Let's go outside and sit," he said. They each stood up and walked out the door onto the porch. The porch faced south, and the sun gave way to the night to their left. The orange sky turned purple as the darkness and stars appeared. The moon was overhead. They sat on the bench that had blankets on it for cushions. She leaned in and put her head on his shoulder.

"I can't believe you bought us this plot and house," she said.

"I can't either. The well water was too good to pass on," he said back. Again, he still felt at peace.

"It is good well water. What will we do with all this space?" she asked. In her excitement, she asked him this often, looking for no answer.

"Fix the fence for the horses. And see about some hens. A nice garden over there." He pointed to the grassy area east of the house that had some shade from trees. "What do you think?"

"Oh, that makes me think of Maple," she said. "I miss her."

"She was a good horse," he humored her. The horse broke its leg in a prairie dog hole on their way west. There were smarter horses in the world than that one, but that horse was special to Ora, so he humored her. They had gotten a new horse when they reached a ranch. It was a black younger horse. It had not erased the memory of Maple.

"She was. Everett, I like your ideas," Ora said to him tenderly.

"Thank you, what would you like?" he said back to her. The crickets chirped in the distance.

"I have one wish."

"What is it?"

"It isn't what you would expect. It is silly," she said with all this vulnerability.

"Tell me," he said, listening to her intently.

"I want to open an orphanage," she said to him.

Everett looked at her and sat in silence for a few moments. "Well, we have the space for it." He pointed to a place in the distance. "What about over there?" He didn't expect this at all.

"Next to the tree," she said back to him. "That would be perfect." She turned and kissed him.

"Why an orphanage?" he asked her, looking at her eyes. He saw the reflection of the moon in them. He thought he knew why.

"I don't want kids growing up like I did, without hope," she said. He smiled at her.

"We will need to get building one then," he said, looking out toward the elm tree.

"You don't mind?" Ora asked him. "If you do, just tell me."

He turned and looked at her. It was much darker now, and the sun had set, and the stars lit up across the sky. "I don't mind," he said to her.

"Good," she said back to him. "What has been your favorite part of our travels?"

"Your sarcasm," he said back to her with a laugh; his eyes were still on the range in distance. She hit his arm and sighed.

"Glad, I can entertain you," she snapped backed. "But be honest."

"Besides this," he said holding her, "taking the river boat to the Mississippi from Ohio."

"That had been so much fun. You taught me how to play cards," she said.

"You were a quick study, didn't dent my pocketbook any," he said back as he put his fork down.

"We were so out of place," she said. "They had good gin and vodka."

"I drank bourbon for three straight days," he said. "Just a rough cowboy and small-town girl with city folks."

"You aren't that rough, but I did finally get you to buy a new pair of pants. Maybe I could get you to go to the barber too," she said back to him.

"The hair stays, woman!" he said back to her. She laughed. He couldn't let her win every battle. "What was your favorite part?"

"I think when you rode into the cottage and I saw your face. Then I saw how you looked at him with a rage I had never seen."

"I was gonna kill that man," he said back to her.

"I know," she said. "Everett, don't lie to me. Have you killed a man before?"

He didn't reply for a long while. "I have."

"In cold blood?" she asked him.

"Everyone that met their end had it coming one way or another. I am no saint. I won't claim salvation or redemption for who I am or what I've done," he said in his voice. There was silence for a long while. She processed this. He looked at her.

"I believed you were a gunfighter, I also know you wouldn't hurt me, but I didn't believe you would kill someone. Why do you live that way?"

"I never went looking for trouble," he said. "It kept finding me. I decided I ought to run into it for once." She watched his face, and he seemed to be outside of his body as he talked. "Are you judging me?" he asked her.

"No, I am not. What did you really do to get all this money, Everett?" she asked him. The moon was high in the sky at this point. "It is more money than Pinkertons make."

He tapped his fingers on his knee and shifted his weight to crack his back. "I am a hired gun. All this came from that."

"You take their land if they don't pay and collect interest on loans?" she asked.

"Yes." The word had to be forced out of his mouth. He didn't want to admit it to himself. He couldn't look at her, so he looked straight ahead.

"You're more than a scoundrel, more than a filthy wolf preying on the weak." She sat up straighter and raised her voice at him. "Don't you want more for yourself?"

"What is there to want?" he said to her back to her.

"Don't you want goodness, wholeness, and joy?" she said back.

"All that is fleeting," he said back to her.

"Circumstances make it convenient to justify your actions. Taking the easy road. Has that quenched your thirst?" she said back to him. "What are you searching for?"

He looked at her with annoyance. "Circumstances, what do you know about it!" He thought of Hawk with Fire's words.

"As much as you. I didn't choose wickedness even if I danced with it for a while," she said back to him.

"You can thank me for that," he snapped back. She was upset and had a tear roll down her right cheek.

"You're right, Everett, you did," she said with another tear. "Let me do the same for you."

"What if you can't?" he said to her. He was vulnerable now and more open than he had ever been. He wasn't buying jewelry, dinners, or land; he was using the most threatening thing to all people. He was trading in the currency of one's soul. These trades are not always paid back in full because they require faith. That faith is not always rewarded.

"I will. I know that because I love you," Ora said to him.

Everett didn't say it. Ora could feel it, but he couldn't say.

Ora said to him, "I know you do. It is eating you up inside to keep going on this trek. Your character is stronger than this."

"You don't walk away from these people," he said. "I can't just stop."

"Yes, you can! How will they find us?" she asked him.

"I have to meet him soon not fifty miles from here next week," he said back to her. "I can leave after the job. We can run away then in a few weeks. We can go to a city. We can have that orphanage there."

"We can't stay here?" she said back to him. "We started a life here."

"We did but leaving changes things. They are dangerous," Everett said dryly. She felt very small.

"I'm not worried. You promised nothing would happen to me," she said.

"I did say that," he said.

"Find a way to keep it then," she said.

Chapter 15

The board room drapes sat open, and the light came through the window. The shadows cast out onto the table from the figures seated around. The air sat heavy and warm. Each man was sweating through his suit as they baked in the heat. A few men smoked their pipes, and this colored the scent of the air with a hint of tobacco. The pitchers of water could not be refilled fast enough as they were drinking them down as fast as they were refilled by assistants. Here in Philadelphia, the most powerful men on the East Coast of America were gathered. They were there because the president had ordered them to solve a problem.

"Hancock, that is a terrible idea," the senator from New Jersey declared. "You're lucky your great granddaddy signed that parchment hanging on the wall, or you would long ago been run out of politics."

"I haven't yet heard from your mouth any trace of gumption that can solve this problem," Hancock replied to Smithe.

"Those are fighting words while I will—" Smithe replied.

"Gentlemen, let's not get sheepish and find ourselves dueling. None of us are a good shot. It is unbecoming of gentleman to succumb to the heat that this July day has brought upon us," the governor said as he cut them off.

"Quite right," Smithe said. Hancock echoed this as well.

"Now, the matter at hand. We have unrest in the western states and territories. Land grants are changing hands, and we have organized crime controlling our towns. This is bad for the country and bad for business. We had a family butchered not long ago for failure to pay land loans. The others just ran off. The bank was forced to sell them for pennies on the dollar to development companies. Holding companies," the governor said.

The other man sighed and jumped into the conversation. Mr. Smithe screamed against the debate and slammed his hand on the table. It makes no sense, the governor thought. I have already won the argument. Now, with the pieces in place, he merely had to make the suggestion, and it would be his. The bickering continued further down the table.

"Now, Representative Clanton, you mentioned the use the military service to stop these renegades. What do you suggest?" Senator Holaday asked. The group became silent as they waited for an answer.

Clanton took a long drink of water and used a handkerchief to wipe the sweat from his brow to gather his thoughts before speaking. "It appears, gentlemen, the western marshals are out of their league. Now, if it was Texas, then by God, we wouldn't have a problem. We would all be at a festival, enjoying dried fruit. Don't judge me. It is my wife's fancy, but I digress. But it's not happening in Texas. It seems to be happening every other patch of dirt but there. Such, there is no dried fruit or festivals to be enjoyed today. Again, I digress, but good Lord, Smithe, blow your nose. Don't wipe it on your sleeve!" Everyone looked at Smithe. He stopped using his sleeve and borrowed a handkerchief from the delegate next to him.

Clanton continued, "I must be digressing because of the heat." He cleared his throat and took another drink. "None of the citizens, even those charged with upholding the law, seem able to exercise their second amendment rights and put an end to this epidemic. We will have to do it for them. We can't have the expansion of this country, not after all the work after the civil war to come crumbling down. To do that, we need force."

The men all cheered this, and others voiced similar opinions as well. Senator Loyrell replied, "Whom do you suggest, the cavalry? The Marines? The Army?"

Clanton jumped back it, "The cavalry, just a bunch of cowards on horses. The Marines, they have sea legs. The Army, it takes them six months to cover twenty miles. I tell you, we need a group of Texans."

Smithe jumped back into the conversation, "Clanton, aren't you a senator of Arkansas?"

"I am," he replied.

"Why are you championing Texas over your own state?" Smithe asked. They all looked back to Clanton in confusion, who was still sweating profusely.

"I enjoy their barbecue and the tea. My citizens are bush whackers, but they don't know the territory and haven't fought worth a damn since the revolution," Stonough said.

"You aren't up for reelection, are you?" another pined in. They all laughed.

"Gentlemen, let's stay the course. Now, all would be fine choices, gentlemen. Texans and Arkansans included. We know they are all capable," the governor said. "Military action would be a bit too direct, and our perpetrators are seemingly shadows. They would go undetected because our force cannot hide by the nature of their uniform."

"What do you suggest then?" Loyrell asked. "Bounty hunters?" he said with a condescending laugh.

"Bounty hunters . . . they are too unreliable and clumsy. They will get sloppy and then talk to the papers. This will lead to more unrest. We need steadfastness and furtiveness so that these thieves won't know what is coming."

All the men seemed to ask in unison, "Do you have a recommendation?"

The governor had to withhold his smile. I won again, he thought to himself. "I do," the governor said. "Mr. Francach, come in." A tall man walked in. He was wearing a long blue jacket, a worn black hat, blue pants, and a red shirt. He walked up to the table and sat down. He had a peculiar mustache. "Gentlemen, this is Mr. Callon Francach. A hidden gem in security and arms community for these kinds of situations in the Pennsylvania region."

One of the representatives asked, "Who are you?"

"Callon Francach, sir. I was a member of the Union cavalry and was honorably discharged several years ago. I handled special assignments for General Tawsen. I was transferred out of Custer's command two months before the massacre."

"General Tawsen, he is a respected fellow," one of the less-important politicians said. "His methods are unorthodox."

"He has great judgment," another said. "Unorthodox methods or not, he is good."

"Why should this committee utilize your services?" another asked.

"Well, sounds like you want to stop these bastards. Tales of two men running amok all over the frontier. If I heard you all correctly, doing that without causing much commotion. I work quick, and I work quiet. My men work quick and quiet. That's why they call me the man in black."

"Your jacket is blue. Why do they call you that?" a different man asked.

"Can we focus on the matter at hand, please?" the governor said.

"The man's jacket is navy blue, and he is called the shadow. We are about to pay the man a fucking large sum of money. I want to make sure he isn't a fool and that this is a serious proposition. Dammit, man, think of the taxpayer," he retorted. The men all laughed.

"Think of the taxpayer!" they said as some of them drank $50-a-bottle wine. (That is a $1,200 bottle in today's money.) Francach stood there like he could care less what these men said about him. He took out a flask and sipped on some bourbon.

Another jumped in and asked, "So it will be you, Mr. Francach, and how many others?"

"No, I have a group of four men." The men nodded in agreement. Francach continued, "Gentlemen, I will have these men for you within three months' time. We can even bring them in alive for you if you want. A public hanging can do some things to preserve the natural order of things. Like this" Francach turned to the man that mentioned his jacket being navy blue and drew a pistol from under his jacket and pointed it at him.

Everyone gasped. The governor grinned. A different politician screamed out, "How did he get a gun in here?"

"I told you, I work discreetly. Now, do I need to pull this trigger, or are you gonna set me loose?"

"The man has a point. He works discreetly, and his methods are unorthodox. Though this may be extortion," he said.

"Yes, yes, he does. I think you are our man," said the politician who had the gun pointed at his head. He pissed himself under the table. "You definitely learned from Towsen."

The governor called for a vote. It came back unanimously in favor of using Mr. Francach. The governor said, "Well, I believe you are our man. Thank you, Mr. Francach. The information will be in a file at the hotel on 6th Street for you with a small advance."

Francach didn't smile. He lowered the gun and put it in his holster. He laughed and smiled and walked back out. The door closed, and one of the men said, "Where did you find him?"

"We have used him when necessary for a period of time," he said. "There were some labor issues in Philadelphia, and they were made to go away."

"I'm still wondering why they call him the man in black, with that awful navy jacket," the man replied. He was still pale from the revolver being pointed at him and having pissed-soaked pants.

The governor scoffed, "The man is color-blind, Orville, dammit. It looks black to him. Must we discriminate against those with a disability?"

"Color-blind?" he replied.

"How did you win office?" Representative Bush said. "You're an idiot."

"Because his last name is Kennedy," another chimed in. The others laughed, and the meeting continued. "Never worked a day in his life."

"It's true," Kennedy said. They all laughed.

"Thank you, gentlemen, for your time. I will see you in the parlor at eight this evening for brandy and billiards," the governor said to them. He shook all their hands. The side conversations continued. One of the men joked that they would be able to eat dried fruit now. The governor walked out into the hallway and turned to walk to his office. He opened the door to his office and found Francach sitting in the chair. He had out knife and was spinning it using the point on his hand.

"It is good to see you, cousin," the governor said. "They have no idea you were in my office. Nice work with the revolver."

"Same to you," he replied. "Thank you."

"You have some hunting to do. Now, I need you to wire to Tempe for him to be aware of this as well. He will help your search in the southwest."

"He is a good man. I will leave tomorrow. That is a three-week ride."

"Election season is coming up. I want to nail these bastards. I mean really get them. The people will love it. Just be steady because by the sounds of it,"

"They haven't met me," Francach replied.

"They will soon. Now here is the advancement. Ten thousand dollars for you. Steadfast as always."

"Steadfast. Thank you, Governor."

"Thank you, Francach, and give my best to Betsy."

"I will," Francach replied. He stepped out the door and began walking down the hallway out of the building.

"Francach, before you go," the governor said as Francach came back into the office, "remember to keep it clean and quiet like we always do. The papers don't need wind of the action. You have full authority but keep it quiet."

"Yes, sir, just like that pickle in Tallahassee," Francach said.

"Just like that," he replied with a smile. Francach nodded and walked out. Several minutes went by, and the governor sat in his chair and rubbed his temples. Dealing with this small secret national security issue had become exhausting. He walked over to the dry bar and poured himself a glass of Scotch out of the canister. He had to help get these men deal with the problem out west. He was third-generation wealthy, and he himself owned some property on the frontier and farms that helped grow his fortune and foundation. It was in his interests to protect them. It was important to protect the working man as well. It was his duty to the people, even if they were not in his state. He would run for president one day, and this would be a large step in that direction. "I will be a hell of a president one day," he said to himself. He took a drink of his Scotch, and it refreshed him. It was only two in the afternoon. This was rare. He looked out the window and took another sip. He felt something in his mouth and spit out the Scotch. A fly had landed in his drink. He looked at the glass, drank the remaining down, and poured himself another. "Bastard tried to ruin my Scotch," he said with a laugh.

Chapter 16

Everett had woken early the morning two days earlier. It had been cold out, and he carried with him an extra blanket and a long rugged down coat. He wouldn't need it during the day, he thought, but he had been glad to have it in the evening. It was a long ride to meet the man. It had been six weeks since their last bit of work together.

He thought of Ora in that moment, and then he cursed himself for involving someone so good in any of this. Their conversation ran through his head constantly. The metal on his hip called out to his soul, and he had done all he could to resist its temptation. All the good he had experienced hadn't cleaned out the pit that sat in his chest.

It was on the morning of the third after beginning the ride. His horse slowly continued through a patch of uneven rocky ground. His eyes studied the countryside to prevent him and his horse from peril. How his own care for himself would not have caused him to do this, she had made him reconnect with himself, his mortality. Off across in the direction of the sun, he saw the body of a hawk on the ground. Its head kept poking and pulling up skin. The hawk stopped and looked at him. He could see the dead snake it held in its talons. The hawk dared him with his eyes to take his meal. Everett stared back at him and returned his eyes to the road. Soon, they made their way out of the rocky ground and down into a valley that opened to a grassy prairie There was a town out on the horizon. He kicked the horse with his spurs to gather more speed.

Out in front of the saloon sat Vernon. He had a devil of a smile and his teeth showed as it widened as Gunn reached the saloon.

"Well, well . . ." Vernon said. "I was beginning to think I would be undertaking this alone."

"You would like that too much," Gunn said. "I passed through the foothills, lost damn near half a day."

Vernon pointed his finger at him and shook it as he shook his head. He stood up and walked over to shake his hand. "It's best to go slow in those kind of things." He shook his hand. The iron was calling Gunn on his side.

"What is the work looking?" Gunn said.

"Some you will be glad to not have missed. I need your temperament for this type of engagement." Vernon began mounting his horse. The look in his eye turned cold. "There will be more of them than us, and I am going in alone."

"Aren't we always on the losing side of numbers?" he joked as he dismounted from his horse.

"We work best that way," Vernon said as he kicked his horse, and off they rode out of town. "We are headed out toward Texas. Should take about a day."

It was late morning the next day. Gunn's horse bounded across the prairie. His horse was a few paces ahead of the man. In the distance, sat a cabin on a small hill. Smoke was rising out of its chimney. The people inside were having a late breakfast. The horses seemed to move faster as they neared their destination. Their hooves dug deeper into the dirt and hit it a little harder. They pulled up on the reins as they found themselves near. The men tied their horses near the back of the house out of view. Vernon whispered to Gunn, "No one walks alive but who we come to find." Gunn nodded. The iron felt right in his hand as he held the rifle. The sweat fell on his brow.

Gunn walked around to the back of the cabin out of view. He had a pistol on both hips and one tucked into his belt. He flexed his right hand as he waited for the moment to arrive. While this happened, Vernon walked up to the door and opened it to and stepped inside.

There were nine men in the cabin. They were sitting around a long table, eating their breakfast. It smelled of stew and dirty clothes. Vernons knocked on the door frame and stood with his hands up. He cleared his throat and said, "Gentlemen, good morning. I couldn't help myself to paying a visit after smelling this delicious stew."

Each of them looked at him with their weapons pointed at him and cocked. They looked at each other while never looking at each other. It was too tense, too early in the morning for any man to shoot another man.

"I mean no harm. I am just a hungry traveler," he replied. Gunn was still outside. Gunn listened next to the door and had both guns now drawn. His hand was still cramped.

The man reaching for his gun looked back the rest of the group. One of the men with a red shaggy beard nodded. The group had no issue after this.

"There is bowl over there," a short man said. Vernon stepped inside and calmly walked over to the bowl. He picked it up with his left hand and the spoon also in his left hand. The steam rose from the stew.

Another asked him, "What brings you to these parts, mister?"

He did not reply immediately; instead, he put some of the stew into a small bowl. He took some bread and sat at the head of the table on the opposite side as the leader of the group. The man grew impatient and repeated his question more aggressively.

After two bites, Vernon finally replied, "Forgive me, I couldn't think without a bite of food. I am merely passing through from Tempe and will go on to Buxton over the border. I hear they have the finest whores in those parts."

The group laughed at his last remark. The tension that had been building evaporated like rain on desert sand. This incurred a second round of laughter from the men at the table as he made another sly remark. The men went back to their stew and ate and continued talking. Vernon had eaten his fill; he thanked the men for the food. They said, "Glad to help you," or phrases just like that almost all at once, and Vernon even shook a few of their hands as he went back toward the door. It was when he stood in front of the door and turned around that he scratched the side of his head. "Now, gentlemen, could I trouble you for a second bowl of stew?" Vernon asked.

All the men told him to grab a second bowl. He walked over and picked up the same food bowl and filled it back up. "You don't happen to know a good place to eat near Buxton, do you?" he asked after he finished the first bite.

"I would eat at Jeremiah's," one of the men said. "Pretty much anything you eat there will keep you good. Just make sure Old Mary is still the cook."

"Old Mary," Vernon repeated, "I will remember that."

Another chirped in, "Don't listen to that toothless fool. The beer tastes like horse piss."

Yet another jumped in, "I remember you getting right drunk on the stuff about a month ago." All the men were laughing quite heavily. Vernon stood in the doorway and went back to his bowl and poured in some more stew. None seemed offended. The steam was still rising off it.

"Sit back down, friend," one said.

"Thank you, I ought to buy you, gentlemen, some whiskey for the hospitality," he said. "What is in it?" he asked.

"That would be appreciated," he said back.

"This is just rabbit?" a Vernon asked.

"It is all we could find the last few days. It does the job," the man in the light shirt replied. All went back to eating their stew in silence for a few moments. A man with a black shirt in the corner began studying Vernon's face intently. He was trying to place him as if he had seen him before.

"It certainly does," he repeated. It was at this moment he began to notice the men's guard completely drop in the room.

The man with the black shirt who stood behind Thomas asked, "You are a funny man. You rode several days to visit a whorehouse. I think you're a liar, except I am not sure if what you are hiding is good or bad."

The other men began looking back at him, and each stood straighter in their chair. It grew quiet. "No, I just really like a good whorehouse. Who doesn't?" he said. They all laughed, and their remaining suspicions shrank. As he was saying this, he had slipped his right hand under the table. He moved his pistol on his lap and cocked it while the men were laughing.

At this moment, Gunn burst into the cabin with his pistols drawn and fired nine shots into the crowd of men. The room filled with screams, smoke, and the smell of gunpowder. Blood was everywhere. Vernon drew his pistol at the same time and shot the man in the black in the right leg as he had not been shot. The man was stunned. It didn't kill him, and he collapsed onto the group in pain. He kicked the ground, rolling around in pain. Screaming pain, he began cursing out Gunn and Vernon as he held his leg, trying to stop the bleeding.

"I wouldn't worry about that, Thomas," Vernon said.

"How do you know my name!" he retorted. He raised his head and stared into his eyes.

"Thomas, I am insulted. Your beard, it is famous from all the wanted posters," Vernon said mockingly.

"Fuck you!" Thomas spit at the man's face. Gunn stood to his left and began reloading his guns. You could hear the death rattle in the background as several men began choking on their own blood before passing. Gunn walked to the back of the room and made himself a bowl of stew as the conversation continued.

The man wiped the spit from his face with a handkerchief. "What manners," he said with and took out his gun and shot him in the unwounded leg just below the knee. Thomas screamed in pain. "Now, Thomas, you are not going to be walking out of here. I know you robbed the bank near Buxton. You stole $50,000 from our employer and burned a cattle ranch that he owned as well."

"I am not going to tell you shit," the man said. The blood was pooling on the floor. Gunn continued to eat his stew and was chewing the meat very hard. There was a small bone he felt with his tongue and spit it onto the floor. He looked to his right, and a finger was on the table that had been shot off. He flicked it onto the ground.

"Quit making a mess, Gunn," Vernon said to Gunn. "Now . . . Thomas, we can make this much less painful for you if you tell me where the money is," Vernon said. He said this as pulled up a chair, turned it around, and sat down in it. He began to reload his gun as well.

"Rot in hell!" Thomas retorted.

"Thomas, I know your family lives not far from Richmond on a farm. Your wife is Mary, and you have two boys, Robert and Marcus. Don't make this painful for them too."

The blood continued to pool onto the floor. "They have nothing to do with this. Leave them be!" he said between painful breaths.

"If you don't tell me where that money is, I certainly will. It definitely won't be quick either. Matter of fact, my colleague here will probably take care of it for me, and as you can see, he is very handy with a gun," the man said with a devilish smile. "And a knife," he added. He took his hat off his head and ran his hand through his hair. Gunn looked at him and waved with a coy smile at him.

"The money . . . is in a box . . . located in the barn at the Totter-Arthur ranch thirteen miles away."

"Wise decision." Vernon stood up and walked out. "Thank you for breakfast, Thomas," he said as he exited. Gunn took one last bite and followed him out. He didn't say a word the entire time.

"Aren't you gonna help me to my horse?" Thomas cried out toward them.

"I assumed you would walk yourself out." He laughed. "Excuse me, I meant crawl," he replied and looked back as Thomas dragged himself outside.

"Fuck you!" he said back to him. "You won't find that money without me coming with you."

Both men laughed at him as he lay there. Gunn went back inside and took handkerchiefs off two men and tied the wounds to slow the bleeding before helping him stand. Thomas raised his leg into the stirrup and Gunn pushed him up over the horse so he could mount it.

The man leaned against the pole on the porch and watched in amusement. He began taunting Thomas about how graceful he was getting up on his horse. The other two mounted their horses behind him. Thomas pulled the reins and led his horse toward the farm. Gunn and Vernon rode behind him about three horse lengths behind. Gunn's pistols were on the front of his saddle to use if Thomas decided to play hero. The glare reflected brightly off the nickel plating. The pistols on his belt were black long-barrel Colt Navy models.

The flaps of their jackets flapped hard as they were riding into the wind through a sea of grass. The heat from the prairie bounced back toward the sky. They reached a small river and stopped to let the horses drink. Thomas stayed on his horse as it lowered its head into the river. Its hair fell over its eyes, and it drank from the cool flowing water. They were not moving fast intentionally to allow darkness to fall.

Gunn dipped his handkerchief into the waters and wiped his brow. He did this a second time, this time getting the sweat off his neck. Vernon stood looking east; his shadow was in front of him as the sun beat onto their back in the early afternoon.

"How much farther?" Vernon asked.

Gunn offered Thomas the canteen. He took a long drink. Water spilled out of his mouth as he tried to swallow too quickly. He took a second drink and put his middle finger up toward the man.

"We have several more miles before we reach it," Thomas replied as he wiped the sweat from his forehead under his hat.

"Thomas, profanity is not going to improve your situation," Vernon quipped.

Thomas took a third drink out of the canteen and flipped Vernon off a second time.

The man drew, and the bullet whizzed past Thomas's ear, barely catching it to leave a mark. "My aim won't be as forgiving next time," he said.

Gunn was not amused at this point. He took the canteen back from Thomas. He crouched along the bank to fill it up. Thomas drank most of the water. This irritated Gunn as he didn't want to get his boots muddy. They each mounted their horses, and Thomas led them toward the farm. This time, they were farther behind as they could tell his riding was less focused as he had become tired from his injuries.

"Let's not risk losing the money by shooting the man in the head who knows where it is," Gunn said to him quietly. He had pulled his horse next to Louis's horse.

"Don't question my judgment," he replied as he looked at him with pale eyes. "I know where this farm is located. I killed his partner that helped him hide it two weeks ago," he said to him quietly. Gunn stared at him, caught by surprise. As their horses continued on, Gunn's expression showed disbelief. He was opening his mouth to ask a question but got caught off.

"He beat me in a poker game about six years ago in Knoxville. When I got his name from his partner, I decided to have a little fun on the job."

"That is a hell of a grudge. You hold on to 'em?" Gunn asked rather between glances forward back up to Thomas.

"Most of the time . . . for the thrill of it," he said with a laugh before he raced ahead toward Thomas's horse. This was the first time where he actually was afraid of Vernon. Gunn felt out of sorts but did not let his facial expression change. He was being tested all the time.

Finally, they arrived at the farm. It was hot and near sunset. Vernon told Thomas to call out as they rode up. Vernon and Gunn stayed back slightly. The man took out his rifle and dismounted. He took cover behind a tree and pointed the rifle at the house. Gunn found cover behind the stone that surrounded the well. Thomas said hello and a farmer stepped out onto the porch. It was Thomas's brother-in-law, Merle.

"Thomas, are you okay?" Merle said. "You look shot up," he said concerned. "Maxwell, come out here," he called for his other brother that shared the ranch with him. Each had pistols on their belts and was carrying long-barrel shotguns, too, as they were preparing to hunt some birds for dinner. Maxwell took a step out onto the porch from inside the house. His hat was tilted to the side.

Thomas yelled, "Run, they got a gu—" Before he could finish his sentence, a bullet split his head down the middle from back to front. His body sloped over the front of the horse, and it began to trot off with the body hanging lifelessly to the right side of the horse. Maxwell and Merle found cover behind large wooden boxes used as flowerpots. The women and children inside the house began to scream.

Gunn sat back and watched from behind his cover. This was different from their normal work, and he felt a tug inside of himself. The iron still called him, but it felt like a hot iron in his hands, burning. He hesitated to fire until a bullet zoomed past his ear. He thought of Ora and knew he wanted to see her again. He peeked over and returned fire on instinct. After firing three shots, Everett looked over at Vernon. He seemed to welcome it and revel in the danger. There was a stench that was coming off him that seemed inhuman. This was not business but revenge. He began to laugh and then stick his head up to return fire. Gunn fired and ran up to a wagon for cover. They were going to get them with cross fire.

"Emma, get the kids to the barn!" Maxwell screamed. The family inside was screaming in the carnage. A few moments later, from the rear of the house, a woman and two children ran low toward the barn. Vernon shot at them twice. Gunn paused and couldn't fire on them. One shot grazed the woman in the right shoulder. Gunn chose to fire off a few shots in their direction but missed wide enough to make it seem like he wanted to hit. The children were crying and screaming in the chaos. Vernon had stood up to make the shot, and one of the brothers' bullets found his right side. He crumpled over in pain. He gathered himself enough and returned fire. It struck Merle in the back while he was trying to make the house. He collapsed and crawled into the house. Maxwell ran and made the house but was shot through the leg. With both men incapacitated, Vernon with his cold eyes looked at Gunn.

"Take care of the family in the barn," Thomas commanded as he looked at Gunn. A look of pure, unexplainable evil came over his eyes. His voice sounded calm as a feather.

"What?" Gunn asked him.

"You heard me!" Vernon said back to him as he dropped his rifle and pulled out his pistol with his right hand and a knife with his left. He walked slowly toward the house. Gunn didn't question this and walked toward the barn. His head began to spin, but he kept focus. The iron scolded him in his hand. Everett neared the barn. The light from the sunset cast into the barn through the door. In the corner of the barn, he heard the woman and children whispering. He walked up to them and drew his pistols. His hands ached. The family held each other and looked up at him. In the background from the house, they could hear the men screaming in pain. Tears fell from Gunn's eyes as he pointed the pistol at them. As he tightened his fingers on the trigger, his eyes looked into the mother's eyes. The world slowed down. He pointed the pistol away from them and put his finger up to his mouth and shushed them. He whispered to them, "I won't hurt you."

The mother looked at him and saw honesty, saw mercy. He saw thankfulness and thankfulness in her eyes. She pushed her children toward the pile of hay in between the animals. There were still cries coming from inside the house, but not it was only one of the brothers. Gunn fired his pistol into the ground six times in a staggered manner. He turned and walked out of the barn. He wiped the tear from his eyes and walked up to the house as he gathered his emotions. He reached the porch and saw the blood on the floorboards. He saw Merle's body inside the parlor; he had been shot several times and stabbed with a knife. His lifeless eyes were open and looked up at him because his head was tilted back. Gunn put his hands on Merle's chest and wiped some of the blood onto his hands to increase the belief of his brutality in Vernon's eyes.

The other brother was on the floor in the kitchen. Vernon was seated at the table with two glasses and a bottle of whiskey. He had poured himself a glass.

"They hid the money in the hutch," Vernon said calmly. He took a drink. He looked up at Everett. "How did it go in the barn?"

"It went quick," Everett lied. He sat down and took the bottle and poured himself a glass. He took a sip. To appear calm, he raised his glass, and Vernon joined him as they clinked their glasses.

"Good, I wish you would've used a blade instead," Vernon said as he looked up at him. Vernon threw a tin container on the table he had been holding under the table. It had blood on it from Vernon's hands. Everett opened the container, and inside it was $43,000. "They lied about it. That really pissed me off."

Shocked, Everett asked him, "You knew it wasn't in the barn?"

"Yes, his partner said it was in the kitchen inside the hutch. I hate being lied to," he said this and looked into Everett's eyes. Everett did not flinch.

"I do too," Everett said back to him. The men studied each other. Vernon saw the blood on his hands, and this confirmed to him, though falsely, that Everett had indeed done what he was told.

"Good job," Vernon said, and he set his glass down and put his hand into the container and took this money out of it.

"This right here belongs to us. We are splitting it." He took what appeared to be half the stack toward Gunn. Gunn was shocked and looked at the money. "Was this a test?" he thought. Gunn set down the glass and wiped the blood off his hands on the white table cloth.

"All right," Gunn said as he wiped the blood on a towel. He took the money and put it in his coat pocket. He took out his gun and put it on the table and poured himself another glass of whiskey. He picked up the glass with this right hand. The Colt Navy, his smaller pistol, was on the table between both men. Vernon looked at it as well. He poured himself another drink.

"Gunn, you showed me something today." Vernon nodded a few times as he said it. "I didn't know how you would react. I think it's time for you to take a trip with me. In a few weeks, I have a meeting with the big man that runs this whole show. You should be there."

"Where is it?" Everett asked.

"I will tell you in town tomorrow. It is on May 23rd," he replied. Both men took long sips to finish their glasses at almost the same time.

"I'll be there," Gunn said. "Let's get a move on."

"We should, these people deserve a good night's sleep." Vernon stood up and walked over to the hallway. Everett pushed his chair away and followed him down the hall. They got out to the porch, and both men walked toward their horses. The grass was longer, and the dew started to form. Vernon picked up his rifle in the grass. Everett looked around and couldn't find his.

"It may take me a minute. You go on ahead. I will catch up after I find my rifle," Gunn said to him.

"All right, good luck, but not like you can't afford a new one," Vernon said.

"It's sentimental," he replied. "A good friend gave it to me," he lied.

"Sentimental, huh? Well, shit, find it then. I will see you at the ranch. Maybe you left it in the barn," Vernon said with a wink and as he rode away.

Everett knew where his rifle was. It was in the tall grass over to his left. It called to him. He walked over toward the barn and kept looking to make sure Vernon was gone now. He stepped inside and walked over to the hay. The woman and children were not making a sound. He took two thousand dollars out of his pocket and laid it on the floor. She made eye contact with him and saw he motioned to be silent. He left without making a sound.

Everett went over to the tall grass and pretended to be looking for the rifle until he "found" it. He picked up his rifle back in the grass and holstered it. He put on his coat and took a drink of water from his canteen after he mounted his horse. The moon was high in the sky, and the stars spread across the sky lit the path back to the ranch. He took his time and put on his gloves to keep his hands warm. He felt dirty, not from the blood and sweat but from the gravity of his decision to join up with his man, to live this life and bring about these consequences into existence. It had beaten him in a shape that no longer felt comfortable. His back, hands, hip, and soul ached. He thought of Ora and their time together. "I don't deserve her," he said under his breathe.

On his ride back, he heard the river to his left beyond a berm and trees. He stopped his horse when he saw an opening down to the river. He tied the horse to a tree and took off his boots on the bank, then his pants, and finally his shirt. He stepped into the sand and muddy riverbank and felt the cool water run over his feet. He went in toward his hips, and he lost his breath from the cool water. He went in up to his shoulders. He dunked his head underwater and pulled it back up. The rocks on the bottom were smooth on his feet. He looked to the sky and found a constellation. He kept his gaze on the stars as he walked out of the water onto the riverbank. He took his time and sat on the bank, naked. A broken man, he could still see the blood on his hands. He thought of the family whose lives they had just destroyed. "Life is what you make of it," Ora told him. Besides her, he hadn't done much of anything for anybody other than himself for a very long time.

Here on the riverbank, he finally knew what hope meant and what living was. He said out loud to himself, "Hope, what a fucking thing." He stood up and threw his rifle into the river. He watched it sink a bit and be carried away by the current. He washed his hands and face on the bank a second time. Then he put his clothes back on, and he fell asleep under the stars tonight. He was cold, but that was all right.

Chapter 17

Riding back to town, he looked at his hands holding the reins. They were calloused and scarred. The red sunrise warmed his face, and he could faintly hear a hawk in the distance calling out. He wondered if that was the same hawk from before. He looked down at his hands and squeezed his fingers into a tight fist. They felt at peace.

I am no chisel, no machine, he thought. He looked back up to the prairie in front of him; it was open but for a tree he was riding toward. He did not need to go back to this life. He had found hope the night before. Hope for a life with self-direction and purpose to something besides himself where hatred would not rule his mind or his heart. His horse let out its desire to ride again, but Everett held him in place under the tree once they had reached it. He was breathing heavily and had to allow himself to do so. The horse voiced his displeasure again. He pulled back on the reins and said no to the horse. The horse would have none of it and reared back. Gunn screamed, "Heel." The horse calmed itself, and he ran his hand on the side of its neck to calm the horse. The horse began to breathe more slowly. He began to breathe more slowly. "Relax," he said to the horse. He wasn't sure if he was speaking to the horse or himself. They stood under the tree.

He knew he had to make up time, and now he pushed the horse by kicking his spurs into its sides. It galloped harder than it had in some time. He saw the town up ahead, and he eased back on the reins and let it trot into the town. His back ached, and he adjusted himself in the saddle. He found the saloon and stopped the horse. He tied it in front of the trough, and the horse began to drink. He went inside the saloon. There were only two patrons in the bar, and each sat alone on the far side.

"What would you like stranger?" the bartender asked.

"I think I will have some water," Gunn said. He was sweating and felt uneasy.

"No water, just gin and whiskey," the bartender replied.

"Gin then," Gunn said back to him. The bartender took a glass and poured some gin into the glass and then tapped the bar. Gunn looked at the sign, and it read three pieces for a glass. Gunn took out the change and paid for the drink. The patrons looked over at him. Gunn went to drink the glass but held it to his mouth. He couldn't drink it. He set it back down. The patrons looked over at him again. He turned and walked back toward the door.

"Aren't you going to drink your gin?" the bartender asked him.

"No, I am not," Gunn said as he walked outside. He walked up to the horse trough and splashed the water onto his face. He took some of the water with his hand and drank the filthy water. He took his handkerchief and wiped the sweat from this forehead after he lifted his hat. He stood up.

"My word, Everett Gunn, drinking from a horse trough? You must be having a hell of a bad day," Vernon said from behind him. Everett looked up and could see his shadow in front of him of the wide, unbent brim of his hat.

"It's been a rough morning," Gunn said back to him. He turned and looked at Louis. Vernon had on a nice black suit and long jacket. His shirt had a slight cream color from the dust on it.

"Stand up, you scallywag, and let's get a drink. You need your wits about you," Vernon said to him. He extended his hand and helped Gunn rise to his feet. Water was still on his face. Vernon patted him on the back, and they walked back into the bar. The two patrons and bartender both looked back at Gunn.

Vernon put up his hand and said, "Two whiskeys."

The bartender looked at Everett and said, "Is he gonna finish this time?"

"What do you mean?" Vernon asked the bartender.

"This fella ordered and paid and just walked outside. Didn't take a sip—" the bartender said.

Gunn cut him off, "Just pour the damn whiskey."

"Okay," the bartender replied. He poured the whiskey into the glasses and corked the bottle. Vernon paid the bartender. Each man took a glass.

"Let's go sit over there," Vernon said as he pointed to a table that was empty in the far corner of the room. He led Everett as they walked over to the table. The patrons paid them no mind. They sat on opposite sites the table. They raise their glasses and then took a drink.

"What is our business for this trip?" Everett asked.

Vernon took another drink. "There is no business other than discussing the arrangements for our meeting with the employer. I was wrong; we have two weeks' time to meet in Northeast Texas. Town will be Sand River Gorge. There is a hotel there called the Good Night Stay. We have our meeting set for the 23rd at 11:00 a.m. Do not be late."

"Not even fashionably." Everett chuckled to break the tension.

"Clever, I wouldn't be late even in your Sunday best."

"All right, I will see you there that morning then," he said back.

"Good, I see you have a nice ranch not far from here," Vernon said to him.

Gunn felt his anger become focused again and his blood pressure rose. He raised the drink with his right hand and remained calm waiting for Vernon to probe. "I do, nice bit of land."

"Smart decision to find a place to lay down your head," Vernon said. "Don't put down too deep of roots."

"I wouldn't worry about that," he said back to him.

"Good. I rode by the other day. There was a woman out on the porch," Vernon said. He studied Everett's response.

"A man needs company from time to time," he said back to him. Vernon laughed and patted him on the back.

"Helps pass the time," he said. "I started to worry for a second." Both laughed. "I ought to come by sometime."

Everett knew he was testing him, and he didn't hesitate, "Anytime you feel the need. I only got one bed though and ain't much for sharing."

Vernon studied him and laughed again. "It will have to be next time. I have some affairs to attend to up north."

"Next time then," Everett said back to him.

Vernon got up and shook his hand, and he walked out of the bar. Everett sat and watched him leave. He thought of Ora and knew the danger she was in at this point. He finally stood up, and his shot of gin was still on the bar.

The bartender said to him as Gunn looked at it. "You drink like a Yankee."

Gunn looked at him and downed the shot. He slammed down the glass and slid it down the bar toward him. "Yeah, you pour like a woman."

Chapter 18

He had arrived back at the house after the attack on the family at the farm. It was in the morning, and the air was still cool from the night before. There was no wind that morning, and the air just sank. He put his horse away and walked into the house. He kissed her when he got inside the house. Ora had missed him while he was gone and worried the entire time Everett wouldn't return in a cruel bit of luck. He lay down and took a nap. He was asleep, and she lay down next to him. He didn't speak much to her for a few hours. The silence spoke for them, and she could feel something was amiss.

It was late morning on his second day since returning. Ora said, "I am sorry for fighting with you before you left."

He sat in the chair on the table as she sat across from him. He spoke softly, "You were right, Ora." He admitted defeat to her. "This shit eats you and swallows your soul."

She leaned toward him. "What happened?" she asked him. "What did you do for all that money you brought back in your jacket?" she asked without accusing him. She waited for his answer and waited eagerly for his answer.

"The guns, it feels right," he said. "Always felt right. I can almost hear the thing speak, and it fills me up. This empty pit." He pointed to his chest. Ora felt empathy for him as a lost soul. He was lost. Everett continued on, "A man wronged my partner and came back around after robbing the wrong bank," he said. "I met my partner, and we rode to a small shelter where this man was. A group of men were in there." He paused before continuing, "We gunned them down for taking money from the man my partner works for." He said this and a tear fell his cheek. "That led us to a farm to collect the money. He butchered the men inside, and a woman and children ran into the barn." He had to swallow before he continued, "I followed them in there and drew my gun." He stopped before continuing. Ora gasped and couldn't breathe as she waited for him to continue. "I couldn't do it, I couldn't shoot them. I left them to get away after we left."

She stared at him across the table and said in French, "Women and children, Everett, I know you have done terrible things, but you're not that person. I don't judge you for it."

He looked at her and threw the money on the floor. "That there is my half. Twenty thousand dollars. I am a contract killer."

She looked at the money and then at him. "You don't have to be."

"I won't be," he said. He noticed her luggage packed next to the bed.

"I thought about leaving," Ora said. Ora had begun packing her things to leave him as she felt abandoned and truly felt he was without saving. They were at the foot of the bed, but she wanted to see him one last time.

"I wouldn't blame you," he said. "You deserve more than a scoundrel."

She said, "You're no scoundrel."

"I think I am," he said. "My partner knows you're here."

"I am not scared," she replied and then smiled.

"Why are you smiling?" he asked her.

"It's just good to have you back," she said to him. He smiled back at her.

"We have to leave together," he said. "We can't just ride out of here, though, because I am sure they are watching the ranch."

"What then?" she asked him.

"You are heading north to Sand River Gorge, you have to catch the train while I am at my meeting," he said.

"Aren't you going to ride it with me?" she asked, angered and concerned. They had walked inside, and he noticed the cases over beside the bed.

"I can't, because I have to go to the meeting so they don't follow you."

Ora said, "I don't understand."

"Ora, if he finds out I didn't kill that woman. He is gonna hunt me and you down. I am not gonna let something happen to you. I am probably already dead," he exclaimed.

"Why is that?" she said.

"Goddammit, I love you. Just listen to me for once," he said for the first time to her out loud.

Tears fell down her face as she couldn't control herself. "You scoundrel." She slapped his face hard and left a red mark on his cheek.

He didn't put his hand on his face. Instead, he picked up the money on the floor and went over to the drawer in the nightstand and opened up a hidden compartment in the back. He took out a black sack and put the money inside. He turned and walked over to her.

"You are gonna leave me after what you just said?" she said.

"It's a day-and-half ride. Take this and go. Start that orphanage," he said. Her heart broke. She slapped him again. This time, he caught her hand and pushed it away. "Don't be like this," he said in French. He felt torn up inside from the hurt he was causing her. He put the money inside the brown leather case. There was $55,000 inside of it for a total of $75,000. He took both cases and carried them out and put them on the small brown wagon that had come with the ranch. "Go stay with the Charles Jones and his family tonight and arrive in town the day after next for the train. All right—"

"I'm not leaving without you," she said back to him before he could finish. She raised her eyebrows, and her face went white. His face grew still as she looked into his eyes. He half-smiled at her. It was all he could do in that moment as he breathed and felt resigned to fate that his deeds might bring the reckoning he knew would come one day but should never come upon her.

"I have to go. You need to go on without me into the town," he said to her as he stepped closer. He kissed her. She began to cry as her heart sank. The tears fell down her cheeks as she felt the chasm form between them. As he held her in his arms, her tears ran down onto his jacket. Inside, he felt totally empty.

"Why are you doing this?" she asked him as she looked into his eyes. They still held in their embrace.

"To protect you," he said in French.

"Funny way of showing it, leaving me for the wolves," she replied. He listened and did not reply.

He kissed her a final time. Then he turned and walked out to his horse as she stood and watched him leave. His footsteps pierced her ears and heart like thunder as she saw him moving farther away.

"So you get to just walk on out me, but I can't walk out on you!" she yelled, trying to hurt him in that moment. "Just go then. Ride out of here after you say you love me, you coward." She ran outside up to him and pushed him toward his horse with both arms with all the force she could muster. He did not budge at all. As she stood in front of him, she began to slap him on the face. He felt the sting of the first and caught her hand on the second.

Her tears were flowing down her face like a summer storm on the prairie. "I hate you," she said as her arm remained in his hand. He let go of her arm and put his first hand in the stirrup. She screamed louder, raising her voice, trying to hurt him as deeply as she could so that he would never come back into her life. He mounted the saddle, and everything began to slow down for both of them.

He turned to look at her as he was on the horse. This did not feel right at all to either of them. She could not understand why he would leave her. He said nothing but tipped his hat and nodded toward her. The sound of the wind over the trees and of the hawk in the sky is all that could be heard. The moment felt like eternity.

As he was about to spur his horse to take off into the town, she said, "I will go to them if you don't turn around right now," she said in a last-ditch effort to get him to stop.

His foot halted, and he turned to look at her. The horse bellowed with impatience. "The hell you will," he said coldly and angrily. A crease formed on his brow that she had not seen. The iron began to call to him, and his hand felt the pull.

He dismounted in a rage and didn't bother to tie up the animal. She had returned to the house and stood on the porch. He had a look she had never seen that was one of pain, anger, and love all at once. His shoulders looked as it carried the weight of the world on in that moment from the tension it displayed.

"The hell I won't," she said. "I'll do what I—" He reached his arms out and embraced her like he never had before and pulled her close and kissed her with a passion she had never experience. She felt his beard on her face, and they continued kissing as he pushed her back up against the wall. He picked her up and carried her into the house over to the bed as her legs were wrapped around her. They tore off each other's clothes and made love for as long as they could. Their hearts were in unison. He held her as she laid her head on his chest after they could no longer. Neither was sure how long they lay there, and neither wanted to leave. Soon it was morning the next day.

Finally, he sat up and looked at her. "You're something, you know that."

"You're a lucky man," she said as he took his hand and moved her hair behind her ear.

"A train leaves tomorrow 11:45 a.m. heading north. I want you to get on it," he said to her. He looked at his watch. It was half past ten in the morning.

"North toward Sand River Gorge? I only will if you come with me, Everett," she said to him. "You're not leaving me." Then she kissed him.

"I won't leave you," he said. "I will find a way to get on the train after I meet them at noon. I promise." He thought of the prospecting going on up north and if he could lie to head there. "I could tell them I will go silver mining, prospecting for them."

"It is simple enough to work," she said. "So you will make the train?"

"I will, I promise. Just have them load your chests into the luggage and buy your ticket. There is a café next to the station."

"I will. Where should I meet you if we get separated?"

"There is a hotel. Stay there, and I will meet you no later than the day after tomorrow," he said as he now had dressed. She lay on the bed, covered only by the blanket. She stood up, wrapped in the wool blanket, and he kissed her.

"Je' t'aime," he said. She repeated the line back to him.

He found his horse outside eating grass, and he mounted it. He looked back and nodded. She saw his smile, and the distress he had shown early was not gone. He kicked the horse and took off. She stood there staring at him as he rode away. She felt chilly standing on, wrapped in the blanket, and went inside. The air stuck to her skin, and she washed herself before putting on her clothes. It was a light-blue dress that had been lying on the wood oak dresser. She fixed her hair in the mirror. It made her feel content and confident in that moment. She took the photograph of her mother and the ring from her that she kept on the nightstand. She folded these in a cloth and placed them in a small bag she placed on the wagon.

She opened the one case with the money and opened the bag. She saw the stacks of money. It was folded and wrinkled and slightly worn. She opened it and began to read it. She held her breath and read it with anticipation.

Ora,

I want you to know.

The money I have given you, I earned in his company to start a life for yourself. Open the orphanage you always talked about. Marry a decent man and raise children. My profession filled the hole in my heart. I can't change the evil I have committed, the people I have killed. I was nothing but an empty soul with a vendetta and a gun. I found peace again when I met you. I found forgiveness. Even more, I found hope in life and felt healed by grace.

The cruelty I see is that the reason I met you was the work that will take me from you. If that is the case, it was worth it. Know that I love you and you made me want to seek righteousness. I ride to this meeting, knowing I will be killed. They do not know you and will kill you as well if they are to learn of our relationship. This was the only way to ensure that you are safe. You must make this train and get out of here to ensure you are safe.

Amour,
Everett

Her hands shook, and she realized why he had tried so hard to leave her the day before. They were both drawn to each other, and fate had brought them together. She knew that his feeling of leaving to protect her had changed and that she had to reach the town. She folded the note and tied the horse to the carriage. She went back inside and put on the hat he had purchased for her, the gloves, and lastly the necklace he had bought her some months back.

She looked at herself in the mirror that sat in the corner. She felt proud of herself and how she had changed so much since meeting him. The last thing she did was take a derringer pistol and place it in her pocket for protection. She walked out to the wagon and rode off toward the town. She looked back briefly at the house and felt the past slip away from her. It felt like the smoothing of a stone in a stream.

As the horse carried her closer to the town, she felt in control and, for the first time, felt that tomorrow would bring a brighter sun than the day before. She finally reached Charles Jones' and the mission when she hit the open field and the last three miles of her journey. She rested there that night.

Chapter 19

In the hotel room, the sunlight shot through the window and brought light to the furniture in the room. On the dark oak table, there was a glass of water that sat on a napkin acting as a coaster. The pitcher of water that had filled the glass sat on the desk near the table. The governor sat on the chair at the table. He tapped his foot to the same impatient rhythm under the table. He reached into his pocket and took out a nickel-plated timepiece. He had bought this from a department store in New York several years before. He put the watch back into his pocket and shifted his weight in the chair. Five long minutes passed, and he checked the watch again. Again, it read the correct time.

Down the hall of the hotel, he heard the faint sound of footsteps along the floorboards. Each faint adjustment of the floor grew louder until he saw certain that the steps head toward the corner room he sat in. The steps stopped in front of the door. The governor turned his chair to face the door now, paying no mind to the heat or his timepiece. The handle on the door rattled before it began to turn. The door began to open, and the governor took a drink from the glass and wiped his mouth with this sleeve. Sweat fell down his brow. In the doorway stood Paul, his assistant, and beside him stood the man in black.

"I apologize, Governor. Took us a minute to get across the town," Paul said to him.

"Luckily, we have time today, Paul. Happy you made it, Callon," the governor said. "I was beginning to think your appetite for the card table had gotten the best of you. He used his arm to stand in the chair as his right knee bothered him from the arthritis."

"Not at all. How is that leg treating you?" Callon asked. He hugged the governor after he shook his hand.

"Sit down, Callon. The leg is not well. The pills from the doctor aren't helping me a whole lot," the governor said. As he replied, Paul poured a second glass of water and placed it on the table. He used a cloth as a coaster to protect the wood. "Thank you, Paul," the governor said to Paul.

"You're welcome, Governor," Paul said to him. Paul turned toward the door and exited the room. Neither men at the table spoke until the door had shut, and they heard the steps down the hall. Callon took a drink and spit out the water.

"This tastes terrible," Callon said to him.

"I remember my first beer," the governor said to him.

"You could've warned me," Callon said to him.

"Would that have helped?" the governor replied with a laugh.

"No, it would not have," Callon said to him.

"What news do you have on your task? I need to report back to the committee in a few weeks' time," the governor asked him.

"News that will make you find interesting," Callon told him. He shifted in his chair and took out a pipe and filled it with tobacco.

"Really, what is this?" the governor said to him.

Callon lit his pipe and shook the match after he lit it and placed it on the table. "You read about the bank robbery about fifty miles from here? The American Continental Bank, that got robbed clean out for about eighty thousand dollars."

"Yes, I remember hearing about it. My holding company owns the regional bank that opened it," the governor said back to him.

"Well, Vernon and his compadre caught up to the band that robbed that place," Collin said.

"They did, I never received word on this," the governor said back to him. "Did they find the money? No one was left alive to recognize them."

"They made a real mess of the whole thing. I figure the guy, who orchestrated the robbery, pissed off Vernon, and he made this job personal. Bloody mess," He said and exhaled smoke into the air.

"Dammit, Vernon is getting reckless with all this. What happened to the money?" the governor said as he pounded his fist once on the arm rest of the table.

"Well, I found about two thousand dollars of it," Callon said to him. He threw it on the table in front of the governor. "Minus my usual percentage."

The governor took the money in his hand and looked at it and threw it back across the table at him. "Keep all of it for the good work. Vernon must have kept the rest. With whom did you discover it?"

"This is where it gets interesting. I found it on one of the bandits' wives about two towns over from where it all went down. About thirty miles," John said.

"Vernon didn't kill all of them?" the governor asked. "That is unlike him."

"Well, before I tied up that lose end, I got her talking and by the sound of it, it don't sound much like Vernon. Must have been the drifter fellow he's been riding with," Callon said. He took another long puff on his cigar.

"Sounds like he has some compassion. Well, he pulled one on Vernon to not get caught," the governor said.

"Vernon kept the rest or they both split it," Callon said. He took another puff on the cigar.

"Vernon and I have an arrangement where there will be some accounting irregularities on certain jobs," the governor said. He looked out the window.

"That may be, Governor, but damn near $80,000 from your bank ain't an accounting irregularity. That is a slap in the face," Callon said to him. He took off the blue jacket and placed it on the chair next to him.

"You are right," he said and then paused. "That is a slap in the face. We plan on eliminating his compadre in a few days correct?" the governor said.

"That is right. Should we just make it two culprits this time? I mean you are gonna be running for the presidency and can't be having loose ends like that running around, right, cousin?" Callon said.

"Callon, you make so much damn sense. He has gotten sloppy, and this mistake in character just proves your point. I have my quarterly meeting with him in two days in town. After I exit the restaurant, wait until you hear the shot that starts it. It will just be Vernon putting a slug in him, then you can put Vernon down as he walks outside," the governor said with dark, cold eyes.

"It will be a pleasure. Seems you will have fortuitous news to report to the committee," Vernon said as he took a long drink of water.

The governor looked at his watch. As the minute hand struck half past, the door opened, and in walked Paul with the lunch he asked to be prepared. They were so busy they had not noticed Paul stepping in, carrying the sandwiches.

"Ah, Paul, this is why I like you. Always arriving at the perfect moment," the governor said.

"Appreciate it, Governor. Here are those sandwiches you requested," Paul said as he placed them on the table.

Callon had stood up and began walking to leave the room as Paul had placed the sandwiches on the table. "Mister Francach, won't you join me for lunch?" the governor asked.

"I think I will, sir," he said back to him. He sat back down in his chair, and they began eating the sandwiches. They each took a bite of their sandwich after it was laid out in front of them. In the corner of the room on the dress was a pair of pants. They were soaking wet and had mud on the lower pant leg. "What happened there?"Callon asked the governor.

The governor finished the bite of sandwich and wiped his mouth. "That is from a boy running into me in front of the restaurant the other day. I went into the mud and whatever he was carrying—I think it was shotgun shells—fell into the street as it flooded."

"You took the worst of that," Callon said.

"I did, I had to save face and not yell at the child," the governor said back.

"Shame, that would ruin good shells," Callon replied as he finished the sandwich.

Chapter 20

The wagon kept pounding forward. The hooves moving the dirt and grass with a simple purpose. As she got to the street, she slowed down, and the wagon began to crawl. She did not know a single person in this town. The people were looking up at her, and some of the men were tipping their hats toward her and whistling at her. She ignored all of them and continued down the street. On her right, she saw the saloon and saw Everett waiting inside. He happened to be looking out the window and seemed anxious. He saw her and smiled out of the corner of his mouth.

She parked the wagon on the side of a white building and tied the horse up to the tie hold. Then she went up to the ticket window, and she purchased two tickets from the clerk, plus the fifty-cent fee for loading her luggage into the car. She made sure to see the cases loaded into one of the secured cars. She tipped the two gentlemen that worked for the railroad and walked across the street to the café.

While waiting for the train to leave, she ordered a coffee and toast. The coffee softened the bread; it was hard because it had been baked that morning. She tried her best to keep the food as her stomach kept turning over in knots. She tapped her foot on the ground to curb the anxiety as there was still a little over an hour until the train was to leave the station. There was still so much commotion near the station, but none of it mattered to her at this point.

Suddenly, she stood up as she remembered to sell the horse and the wagon. She paid and walked down the dusty street to the stable area. There was a person in front of her in line that was paying to have his horse put up for the day. He was an attractive, well-kept, and educated-looking man. He wore fancy clothes, and she could hear him speaking quite eloquently. There was a dangerous vibe she sensed about the man and saw his iron sitting on his right hip. She sensed this man was one of Everett's associates. He put his hand on his hip, and he continued talking with the clerk. She saw the jagged scar on his right hand that Everett had described to her. Her hands tightened nervously.

He turned around after he finished and looked at her with a devilish smile. "Excuse me, miss. You look beautiful," he said.

Ora tried her best to remain composed. "Thank you, sir. That is kind of you." Does he recognize me?" she thought to herself and tried to act naturally.

"I feel like I have met you before. Have we made acquaintances before?" he asked her.

"No, I don't believe we have met. You presume boldly, sir," she replied politely. Every ounce of her wanted to take the pistol in her purse and shoot this man down in the street where he stood. It would be a fitting end, but then she would still not be able to have Everett. She would just find a noose around her neck.

"I apologize, miss. Allow me then to make your acquaintance. I am Malcolm Arthur Sonnette. And your name?" He kept studying her like a predator studies an animal before it attacks.

"My name is Mary Jones," she lied to him to prevent any connection with Everett. She did not blink and borrowed the name from one of the doctor's clients he treated for fever.

"Pleasure to make your acquaintance, Miss Jones." He took her hand and kissed her hand. The clerk in the window watched this, and you could see his disgust with the arrogance of this man. "Are you in town long? We should enjoy a meal together at the saloon later this evening," he said.

"Thank you, sir, but I am only in town for a little longer. I am catching the train." She felt repulsed and scared as his eyes stared at her intently. He was picturing her with her clothes off.

"That is too bad. Well, enjoy your travels." He released her hand as he said this and then walked away.

After he had walked by, she exhaled a sigh of relief and went up to the counter. She told the clerk she would like to sell her horses and the wagon.

"That man is an arrogant ass," the clerk said.

"That is an accurate assessment," she said with a smile.

He offered her twenty dollars, and she accepted. This was a low offer, but she did not care. She thanked the clerk and turned around. From across the street, Vernon was still eying her. She nodded and then continued on her way up the street back to the café to wait for the train. Vernon followed her and his pace matched hers. He crossed the street and caught up to her.

"Miss, I do believe that if your train doesn't leave for a little bit of time, let's fancy a drink together in the saloon at least," he said coyly.

"Sir, I appreciate the offer, but I am not interested," she said graciously but with a raised voice. At this point, they were in front of the saloon. Everett heard her voice and Vernon. He remained calm.

"Miss, now don't be rude and have a drink with a gentleman," he said back.

Sitting inside, Everett stood up from the table calmly. He walked toward the entrance naturally and did not make eye contact with Ora. He turned to the right on the boardwalk. His steps were swift.

"Vernon, how the hell are you?" he said without looking at the woman.

"Gunn, hello. Allow me to introduce you to this pretty woman, Miss Katelyn Jones," he replied.

Gunn took all his strength to hide he knew her. "It is a pleasure, Miss Jones." They looked at each other.

She shook his hand, and she bit her lip as she received a cold greeting for Gunn. "Well, she is clearly in a hurry. Pardon us, we have business to attend to," he said.

Gunn replied, "On your way, miss." She looked at him and now understood his concern from before. She turned and went straight to the café and sat down waiting for the train.

He made slight eye contact with her but restrained himself. He wanted so bad to kill Vernon and flee. The iron called to him, but he knew the governor's guards were in town already at the hotel. This would be futile as they wouldn't get away as the train still had almost an hour to leave. Instead, he walked back into the saloon toward his table, and Vernon joined him. He was sharing stories and looking to make Gunn laugh. He commented on her beauty and looked to see what Gunn would say.

"She is quite a thing," he said.

"She is easy on the eyes," Gunn said back in a detached tone.

"Such a shame. I won't be able to pay her a visit. We will miss the train with this meeting," he said.

"That is a shame," he said back. Inside he boiled over with anger.

At the café, she sat waiting. The server brought her some wine. The heat made her think of when she would jump in the lake as a child to cool off on long summer days. From the other end of the street, a man dressed in a black suit and top hat walked down to the saloon. Two men that walked around him in a circle. They walked and would laugh at his jokes. Further down the street stood a man in a blue suit just sitting on a rocking chair, smoking a pipe.

Chapter 21

T he floor creaked as he walked over towards them. Vernon and Everett stood up and walked towards him. Their spurs rattled as they stepped into the saloon. It was almost eleven.

After greeting one another the governor made a joke about Everett being shorter than Vernon had described him. The governor sat down at a table out of view of the window; Everett and Vernon sat down as well. Everett sat facing the bar and kitchen. Vernon sat facing the rear of the saloon. On the table was a lamp and four place mats. The air was hot and stagnant. The Caldwells sat on either side of the door.

The waitress came over and greeted them, asking if they wanted anything to drink. They said they needed a few minutes. She told them her sister would be serving the food and taking their orders because she had to go help her husband in the kitchen. She then left. Vernon and the governor began discussing accounts and regions.

The governor wanted to be brought up to date on which accounts had paid up, what new operations had been merged. Some new mining operations and mills had been acquired by the trust in recent weeks out west.

"Expansion is a good thing," he said.

"So long as it doesn't cost you a fucking golden goose," Vernon said.

"That is true, and your work in the north with Ed Jackson has been superb."

Vernon thanked him. He had broken a few bones, lit a few fires, and killed a few people over the last few months. Today was finally his payday for the quarter's work.

"Now, tell me about this gentleman right here. Can't you handle things the same anymore," the governor quacked out joking. The men laughed.

"This is Everett Gunn. He came for his initiation. He had been useful in the whole mess since fucking up the robbery on the train nine months prior."

Everett lied, "I enjoyed it much, sir. We made short work of a lot and brought back quite a bit for you."

Vernon added, "He is a real fine shot and cold blooded as they come."

When he said this, there was a peculiar look on the governor's face. Everett caught it, and he wasn't sure if it was approval or sarcasm.

Again, the governor voiced his approval. He would have a new man to make sure the engine would run for this part of the country. It didn't matter how many poor bastards died as long as it wasn't tied back to him.

"I own damn near 15% of the new territories and states in expansion—and 20% of the banks. All are completely untraceable to me through different shell companies," he said proudly. "My legacy will end with the presidency," he added.

Gunn nodded to agree and move the whole thing on.

Everett continued to let the other two do most of the talking. His mind drifted back towards Ora and the train. He knew he had become a liability, and the chance of him walking out the door, much less get on the train, evaporated by the second. He appeared detached and used this as an advantage, only interrupting when necessary or details needed to be changed of certain jobs. Words flew by him like birds.

The plan was to cover the southern end of the territory over the next few months and look for more partners or acquisitions. The job wouldn't change, just the amount of pain or violence inflicted he thought. The iron burned on his side, but he did his best to withhold his disgust with these men.

The sister came over and told them the specials for the afternoon. They were the same as they were that morning. She wore a necklace with a particular pendant on it. The governor stopped and asked her where she had gotten it from. She smiled and said that she had purchased it in Kentucky before heading west. The governor smiled and looked at Vernon. The women called her sister into the kitchen; she told them she would be right back.

The governor had this smile on his face. Everett became curious with the amusement on the other men's faces. Suddenly the governor began speaking French to Vernon thinking Everett wouldn't understand, "You remember that girl from that wild weekend a few years back in Kentucky, and the whole bit. We had ourselves a good time. That filthy bitch kicked and screamed. Man, that was the best lay I ever had. She had on a necklace that looked like that. Shame she kicked so much we had to put her down."

Vernon laughed from his belly. "Didn't you take her two or three times before we set that place on fire."

The governor responded, "It would have been more if it hadn't been for the son who came running in. How did that go? Not well for him if I remember."

The governor and Vernon laughed banging the table with their hands. Vernon placed his gun hand on the table away from his firearm. This was something he told Everett never to do unless you completely trust everyone you are with. He had thought he was following his own rule by placing the gun on the table with friends. He was not amongst friends. Everett smiled but didn't laugh. He understood every word they said to each other. The iron called now.

Everett turned his chair directly toward the two men. He remained composed and had calmly moved his jacket behind his gun while he had shifted the chair. The black metal barely distinguishable from the dark brown and worn holster around his waist. The sister came back to the table at this moment, took their orders, and walked away. Vernon was still laughing because of the story and turned seeing that Gunn was not laughing with the story.

Everett said to them, "I don't know what you said, but a round of drinks to celebrate."

"I like this man," the governor said. "He stays quiet, I like that too."

The two went back to speaking French while Everett went up to the bar and asked the barkeep for three whiskeys and three beers. He poured the shot glasses with whiskey. Everett brought the two shots of whiskey to the table and placed them in front of the Governor and Vernon. He brought the beers over after this. He left his on the counter and walked back over.

"What should we drink to?" Vernon asked.

Everett said in French as he took the glass in his left hand while standing at the bar, "Burned by lightning but never rolled by thunder."

The men looked shocked as they realized he understood what they had said before. They all drank.

Vernon responded back, "I am shocked you speak French? Fucking amazing wouldn't you say."

"It is. Beautiful toast. I may borrow that."

"Feel free," he said in English.

Everett's throat relaxed as he breathed, but his hands tightened. He fought to remain relaxed as his chest felt like collapsing. He narrowed his eyes and turned to the governor and looked at him inquisitively. He shook his head two times with a slight laugh and turned back to the Louis. "I was thinking about that thing you said to me after the train, what was it again?"

Vernon laughed but wondered why he asked for such an obscure reference. "Man, you are a serious son of a bitch from time to time." He turned to the governor, "He's not always like this."

Vernon turned back to Everett still standing at the bar now sipping the beer, "I remember though. We all end up in the ground, some put others there, some are the one's put there, and the rest just fade away."

The governor laughing, "You might be a preacher with words like that."

Vernon quipped, "Thank you governor, I always felt I had that divine touch with my work. At least with that broad I was." Vernon turned to the man, "Not as elegant as your toast I dare say."

Everett came back to the table and sat down without the beer. The other two men began talking, and Everett didn't listen to a word. His back pain left him, and he couldn't taste the whiskey.

Suddenly Vernon said, "Gunn, you forgot your beer."

"I did," he said and stood up. As he reached the bar, he turned around. With the beer in his left hand, he turned slightly enough so that they couldn't tell he had his hand on his pistol with his right hand. He looked at the Caldwells, and each sat reading a paper. They paid them no attention. Vernon and the governor paid him no mind and kept talking business.

Gunn took a drink and said in French after he lowered the glass, "Thunder and lightning as he looked at both the governor and Vernon."

"Yes, yes, thunder and lightning. Not as amusing the second time around, I don't think I will borrow it," the governor said.

Vernon drank his beer with his shooting hand and turned back away from Everett.

At this moment, Everett pulled the hammer back on the gun under his jacket as he took a sip and unholstered the gun under his jacket. None of the other men noticed, not the Caldwells, not Vernon, not the governor. Everett looked at the Caldwells, and neither had the ability to quickly draw and fire their pistol because they had the old army gun belt where the leather pad buckled over the top of it. Both of theirs were buckled. He took one more sip of the beer and said in French, "Now I have a question."

The governor and Vernon looked up at him and Vernon said, "What is the question?"

Everett answered, "Did that woman in Kentucky have brown hair and a blue dress?" His head cocked waiting for their answer as he stared blankly. His finger danced on the trigger in the gun hidden by his jacket.

Both men, stopped. Both surprised, each said "Yes, she did."

"How did you know that?" Vernon asked with a befuddled look on his face in English. As if this detail could possibly be known.

"Lucky guess," Everett said back to them in French. "Women with brown hair, they have a lot of fight in them." He turned his head back toward the bar and took another sip. There was a silence until the Governor interrupted.

"They do," the governor said laughing and smacked Vernon's shoulder. "How did you really know she had brown hair? Have you been in Kentucky much?"

He looked both men in the eye and laughed again. "I have, and that woman . . . she was my wife," he screamed out. He turned quickly and threw his jacket back and extended his pistol. Everett fired a bullet into the Vernon's right lung. The bullet entered through his back and went clean through into the wall. The governor facing Everett and the bar, fell back in his chair onto the floor and ran toward the back of the saloon in a hallway through an exit in the back. Everett then pointed the pistol at the furthest Caldwell away from him who had dropped his paper and went for his holster. Everett fired at him, and the bullet shot through his face just below right eye ball. After he pulled the trigger, Everett pointed his pistol at the taller Caldwell who had his gun half drawn but dropped it because the nerves had caused his hand to shake. Everett pulled the trigger twice and both bullets shot through his chest. He fell back into the wall and onto the floor. The floor boards shook.

Everett turned back to Vernon, who began spitting up blood as he tried to breath. He was slouched over on the table. He was reaching for his own pistol, but Everett shot him in the lower arm disabling it. The two women in the kitchen continued to scream as their restaurant became a massacre. Everett walked over, and with a cold stare, kicked the table away from Vernon who collapsed onto the floor. The gun flew towards the door. Vernon caught himself with his one good arm and rolled over onto his back. Vernon's gaze met Gunn's. Vernon tried to speak but couldn't get out any words.

Everett stood over him and leaned down, "You ripped my fucking world apart you son of a bitch. I'll see you in hell," He pointed his other pistol at him and shot him through the stomach one time and once more in the chest to collapse the other lung. Vernon screamed, the volume shrunk as he continued to cough up blood. Everett stared into his eyes, his cold eyes. Everett turned and walked toward the hallway the Governor ran down. He left Vernon there in pain to bleed out like an animal. The one sister had screamed after the first gunshot, fainted after the next two.

Everett reloaded his Colts as he deliberately walked toward the back of the saloon after the governor. The shell casings fell to the floor, one at a time. In sequence almost like a clock, the hot metal hit the ground. Everett was ravenous but calm.

He took a step, and the other sister interrupted him as she exclaimed, "You're not going to kill the governor, are you?"

The man stopped and paused. He turned to her and spoke, "I ordered two eggs and a steak. You best have those out here when I get back."

Vernon lay there wheezing more slowly now, still coughing up blood in the background. They had a steak for themselves that had already been placed on the grill. The cook heard this and put it on the plate. He cracked two fresh eggs.

The governor had rushed toward the back of the saloon down a long hallway of the rectangular-shaped building. He reached the end of the hallway, but there was no door out of the building, only a door into a large storage room. He went into the room and frankly looked around. All that was inside of it were cans of food, supplies. He had heard the delayed shots from the dining area. Fear crept up from his feet and rested in his chest like a spider crawling in the night. There was nothing to barricade the door, but he saw a shotgun on the shelf next to oak cast barrels. It glowed to him. He grabbed it and loaded it with the two shells he grabbed from a wood box. He crouched and aimed at the door. He grinned and positioned himself across from the door, slightly to the right. He did not feel calm, his heart pounded with excitement.

Gunn looked down the long hallway. The light from one window at the far end, cut through the darkness. Gunn began to step and walk down the hallway now. He suddenly didn't see the floor boards or the wood walls—he saw the cottage. He hadn't thought of it for so long, and he could see in through the door that had been broken off its hinges. He looked down first and saw her leg, and then her lifeless body. He saw her face and her eyes. He came back as stopped in of the door. He breathed and paused outside the door.

Inside the room, the governor looked toward the cottage, where they had beaten and ravaged the woman and how they had left her and the child. He felt no remorse, only agitation at how this day had unfolded and how it may alter his plans for power.

He paused and didn't breathe as the footsteps stopped outside the door. He wanted to look him in the face before he killed him. To let him know he had won. His finger eagerly awaiting to pull back on the trigger. Sweat fell off his brow onto the floor and droplets began to sprinkle themselves over its rough texture.

Gunn thought, here it all is. He kicked open the door open. He saw the governor out of the corner of his eyes with his revolver pointed. He saw the sick twisted smile looking at him with a shotgun raised. He accepted what would come. The governor pulled the trigger, and Everett awaited the pain that would follow. The hammer struck the back of the shell, but nothing happened. The gun mis-fired, and the governor's grin evaporated into disbelief and panic. Gunn's face did not change, nor did he hesitate as he pulled the trigger and fired. The bullet when into the governor's right shoulder area and knocked him back. The second shot went into the knee cap in his left leg. The bone exploded, and pieces shot out across the floor. The governor screamed out in pain, and blood began to drip out onto the floor boards working their way into the crevices and fibers of the wood.

Gunn stood in the doorway with the smoking revolver pointed at the governor. The men stared into each other's eye, the fury and hatred filled the room. Neither spoke, neither needed to. The governor finally bellowed out a grunt of pain, like water leaking out a dam.

The governor gasped as he tried but couldn't straighten his leg. Everett walked two steps closer to him, still pointing the pistol. The sounds of his boots, creaking the floor boards, were the only thing breaking the silence. The governor said, "Is this how you thought it would feel, taking your revenge on the men that killed your family?"

"It feels how it feels," Everett said to him. "You had this coming for a long time."

"Maybe I have, but all that responsibility and pain of revenge resting on you, sounds like a heavy burden," the governor swallowed hard.

Everett stopped now. "I laid my burden down next to the river, in the hills. I made my peace with God. I let that go, but you done dug it up. Now you got the fury."

The governor swallowed again before speaking, "You got a natural way with that thing, this violence. You sure put it to good use." He pointed to the gun and then tapped his wound with his good arm and adjusted his weight to get comfortable. "Seems I gave you direction."

"Not after until that day," he replied.

"Everyman's got a calling," he said.

"Everyone's got an ending too," Gunn replied.

"You sound like a god damn poet." The governor laughed. "Go ahead, kill me. But I'll die a hero, and you'll be just be another outlaw in the west."

"You're right, ain't gonna be fair, but I'll know—and you'll know. That's enough," he replied.

He adjusted his finger on the trigger and pulled it back. He emptied the gun into the chest of the governor and saw his hand drop to the floor and twitch momentarily. The color left his face. He emptied the spent cartridges onto the floor of each revolver. He did not reload either pistol. While he did this, the storage room drifted back to the scene at the cottage. It was spring now, and he saw his wife and child walking outside the cabin. They smiled at him standing inside of it. He could smell the trees and flowers as he exhaled.

Gunn walked out of the room and down the hallway. The call of the steel was gone. There was no pounding, no regret. He felt nothing until he reached the end of the hallway. Breathing became difficult for him, and he felt thirsty. Vernon's body lay motionless next to the table, the chairs around the table still kicked over on the floor. The Caldwells lay motionless. On a table next to the bar was a plate of eggs and a steak. There was a knife and fork next to it on a napkin. He looked back to his left and saw the sister behind the bar. She appeared distressed.

He walked over to the bar and said to her, "Miss, I'd like that jug of tequila right there." He pointed to her with his left hand

"Sure thing, mister," she said and brought it out to him from behind the bar. She went to set it on the table next to the play. Her hands were trembling and shaking as she did this. He grabbed her hand and took the jug from her hand. She looked at him with fear.

"Thank you," he said to her.

"You're welcome," she said. Her limbs didn't move.

"This is for the trouble." With his other hand, he handed her all the money he had in his pocket. It was damn near twenty dollars. Her eyes went wide.

"I'd run along now. The shooting ain't gonna stop just yet."

She nodded and took the money and ran back into the kitchen area.

He took a seat at the table and took a bite of eggs. They tasted good. As he was cutting the steak with the knife, he heard glass shatter and suddenly felt a pain on the outside of his left arm. He felt a warm sensation drip down left side. The blood dropped down onto the floor.

From outside the bar, the man in black had fired through the window a pop shot before the Marshall had gathered order. He had missed his mark and cursed himself for not sighting the rifle more properly. The Marshall scolded him and ordered everyone not to shoot.

"I'll hang you if you pull that shit again," the Marshall said.

Everett almost collapsed onto the floor. He meandered over and rested his back against the bar with the jug. He reached for the plate but could not grab it. He leaned over more and was able to reach a part of the plate with his pinky and nudged it over slowly until he could get a grip on it. He set it in front of him and finished the meal quickly, feverishly cutting up the meat. His hands were no longer calm, shaking as he held the silverware. He began to feel dizzy. The pool of blood grew.

He lifted up the jug and drank a long pull of tequila. He wiped his mouth and looked out dead ahead of himself into the wood slats. Staring at the character of the fibers, he thought of Sarah and Benjamin. His back ached as he sat there so he stood up. His hip ached, and where the bullet had struck him, that pain began to dull.

He said to himself quietly, "Ora get on the fucking train." He thought of the outline of her face, and of the first night he saw her in the bar. A bullet whizzed by him that was fired from across the street that shattered the glass of the front window. It was at this moment he fell back down behind the bar again. This time onto to his side. Small tears came to his eyes.

"Don't fire, don't fire men. You in the bar, come out with your hands up," the voice shouted. Two men over from the Marshall was the man in black. He had fired into the saloon again. "Looks like we may have two hangings, boys."

The life he had wanted had come and gone—and now the life he could have led began to slip away. Everett dried his eyes with his sleeve, and the world began to spin a little bit. He made the sign of the cross on this forehead, and for the first time in a long time, he said a prayer. This was it, this was his lot in life. The natural order of things and though he had taken vengeance, his transgressions had finally caught up with him. His back ached, and he felt tired. He felt gratitude for meeting Ora at least and finding the light.

From across the street, the men outside could see Gunn stand up as a hat rose from behind the bar and begin to walk towards the door from beside the bar. They wouldn't shoot inside because of the Marshall's direction. They called out to him. He walked gingerly and did his best to keep his balance. Everett heard their voices as he looked out of the window while stepping towards the door. There were five of them across the street, probably had one crack shot on the roof of a building he thought. He saw a man in a long blue suit and black hat. Everett knew this was the man they had hired to bring him down, to pin all the heinous acts on him. He would have never made the train

Everett stopped and stepped out of site of the window and the door. He rested against the wall and saw the woman standing behind the bar.

She called out to him, "Mister, why did you shoot those men?"

He looked up at her and said, "I'm just another outlaw in the west." He dipped his hat and walked toward the door of the saloon. He pushed through the double-hinged doors and out onto the street.

The Marshall called out, "We won't use force, if you don't try anything."

Everett stopped outside on the steps of the saloon and walked onto the street. In the distance, he saw a hawk up in the sky. Its wings spread out as it let the wind carry it back and forth. He looked back at the man in black, then up into the sun and felt it warm his face. He glanced down each side of the street. He drew his pistols faster than any man had before. Shots rang out from the deputies and Marshall. Everett staggered forward three paces, dropped his pistols, and collapsed onto the dirt. He caught himself with his right arm, though it was broken from bullets and he rolled onto his back. He coughed up blood and looked toward the sky, no longer able to breathe because his lungs were collapsed. In his last moment, he thought of Ora and the promise he wouldn't be able to keep.

Ora screamed out from the train car as she witnessed it all happen. She stuck her hand out the window as she called out to him as he fell. She began to sob uncontrollably. He had tried to keep his promise, but he had been right. The train pulled away from the station, and it was the last she ever saw of Everett Gunn. She never knew the root of his pain and anguish, but she had seen his redemption and journey back to the light.

Chapter 22

Several years later, the fundraiser event began smoothly. Ora had on a black dress and wore white gloves and a modest necklace. She stood by the door and greeted the patrons and donors as they entered the ballroom. There would be about two hundred people in attendance. She stepped away from the line to use the bathroom. When she returned, the event had start. She found her seat at the front table. The opening speaker thanked everyone for coming that evening. He continued his remarks on the organization and the goodwill it had done in the area. He called Ora up the podium.

Ora stood up from her chair and did her best to hide her nervousness by lightly smiling. She walked up to the podium and thanked everyone again. She made a point to pause and look around the room before continuing. At one table, she noticed the late governor's wife. She was sitting with her new aristocrat husband. This caused her to lose track of her speech momentarily, but she recovered quickly.

"St. Angelo's Orphanage started with modest means. It was a dream I had to help children growing up without their parents to find a place with structure, and as the French say,"je ne sais quo." A person very important to me believed in me and helped make this a reality today. He never got to see what it would become because he is no longer with us. But I will be forever grateful to him, as should everyone in this room." She paused and had to hold back the tears that she knew would come. Without speaking a word, the wife and Ora's eyes met at that moment.

Ora exited the stage and went back to her table as everyone applauded. Many children had benefitted and been adopted by the orphanage since it had been opened.

One of the original benefactors leaned over and asked Ora, "How is your little son, Everett, doing?"

Ora looked at her and said, "He is getting along so well. Thanks for asking. I have one of the sisters watching him tonight."

"Is it true you are teaching him French?" she asked Ora.

"It is. I wanted him to have that connection to my family and his father's family."

"Oh, that is so sweet of you, dear," Mrs. Orthington said.

The speakers continued, and finally the evening began to wind down. Ora walked out to the balcony to overlook the garden and grounds below. She held her glass of champagne in her arm. "You helped build all this," she said under her breath.

"Miss, are you talking to anyone," a lady asked.

"Oh no, just myself, sorry," Ora said. "Hello, I am Ora Gunneth."

"Pleasure to meet you, Ora, and fine speech. I am Mrs. Claude," the late governor's wife said. Ora gasped and almost dropped her drink. "You look like you have seen a ghost," Mrs. Claude said.

"Oh no, just nerves, is all, after my speech," Ora said.

"Whoever helped you start this had quite an impact on you. Was he the father of your child?" she asked.

"He was in fact the father," she replied.

"Good men are so hard to find. I love my current husband, but my Henry, the late governor, he was a great man," she said.

"What happened to him?" Ora asked, already knowing the answer and finding a way to bite her lip. Her face became red, but she breathed.

"A despicable rotten outlaw gunned him down in cold blood. My husband was an American hero. He died at the hands of a bastard," she exclaimed, looking for sympathy.

Ora breathed and thought to herself as she looked at this wealthy woman's pearls, her jewelry, and her expensive dress. It had all been purchased by blood money stolen from hard-working people. She drew in air and looked at her.

"The scoundrel that shot your husband . . ."

She set down her drink.

"Yes, what about him?" she replied.

"That man . . ." she paused to not lose her composure. "That man was the best man I've ever met," Ora said proudly.

About the Author

Josh Turk is an author who grew up forty miles northwest of Chicago in Crystal Lake. He developed a passion for writing and reading of literature during his teenage years after reading John Grisham novels and Ernest Hemingway.

Studying economics and finance in college, he began writing short stories during law school as a way to entertain himself and others from the routine of school. It was here where he began writing his first novel and finished it over the course of four years.

He currently resides in Crystal Lake and works for Intren, LLC.

Made in the USA
Columbia, SC
18 May 2019